"They found us. We have to leave. Now."

Caden grabbed Gwen's hand and helped her up. She could hear men yelling at each other in the middle of the camp, shouting her name. There was no doubt they were looking for her.

Pain shot up her calf as she rushed through the brush with Caden, but she refused to let it slow her down. Those men were armed and, from everything she knew, planned to kill her when they found her.

Caden kept his arm around her, keeping her steady on the rugged path as the voices in the camp faded.

"Where are we going?" she asked.

"There's a shallow spot in the river nearby. We need to cross over, then head downstream on the other side."

And then what? She knew she couldn't keep running. Not for long. She glanced up at his profile as he tightened his arm around her. As much as she didn't like it, Caden O'Callaghan held her life in his hands, and she was going to have to trust him.

Lisa Harris is a Christy Award winner and winner of the Best Inspirational Suspense Novel for 2011 from *RT Book Reviews*. She and her family are missionaries in southern Africa. When she's not working, she loves hanging out with her family, cooking different ethnic dishes, photography and heading into the African bush on safari. For more information about her books and life in Africa, visit her website at lisaharriswrites.com.

Books by Lisa Harris

Love Inspired Suspense

Final Deposit
Stolen Identity
Deadly Safari
Taken
Desperate Escape
Desert Secrets
Fatal Cover-Up
Deadly Exchange
No Place to Hide
Sheltered by the Soldier
Christmas Witness Pursuit
Hostage Rescue

Visit the Author Profile page at Harlequin.com.

HOSTAGE RESCUE

LISA HARRIS

LOVE INSPIRED SUSPENSE
INSPIRATIONAL ROMANCE

LOVE INSPIRED® SUSPENSE
INSPIRATIONAL ROMANCE

Recycling programs
for this product may
not exist in your area.

ISBN-13: 978-1-335-40282-0

Hostage Rescue

Copyright © 2020 by Lisa Harris

This edition published by arrangement with Harlequin Books S.A.

For questions and comments about the quality of this book, please contact us at CustomerService@Harlequin.com.

Love Inspired
22 Adelaide St. West, 40th Floor
Toronto, Ontario M5H 4E3, Canada
www.Harlequin.com

Printed in U.S.A.

He that dwelleth in the secret place of the most High
shall abide under the shadow of the Almighty.
I will say of the Lord, He is my refuge and my fortress:
my God; in him will I trust.
–Psalm 91:1-2

To those needing a refuge and shelter.
May you find it in Him.

ONE

Gwen Ryland held up her phone to take a panoramic photo of the breathtaking canyon spread out in front of her. Even from where she stood, halfway down the steep wall of the chasm, the view was spectacular. She took a string of photos, then turned back toward her brother, her feet slipping on the loose gravel. His hand gripped her arm.

"Hang on, sis." Aaron pulled her back a couple feet from the drop-off. "A photo isn't worth falling off the edge."

"I wasn't going to fall." She laughed away the comment, but that didn't stop her heart from pounding. And while she was still a good four feet from the edge, Aaron was right. A fall here could be deadly. Three months ago, a twenty-year-old hiker had plunged to his death, and his body had finally been recovered two days later at the base of one of the cliffs a quarter of a mile from here. No, she couldn't be too careful. And besides, in all honesty, a photo of the canyon could never do the view justice.

She slipped her phone into her pocket and decided

to simply take in the beauty of the canyon walls. The sunlight cast gray and purple shadows across the wide ravine and impressed them into her memory. Above them, on the top of the deep chasm, was a thick forest of oak trees, while below a scattering of Douglas firs and cottonwoods spread out along the river.

On the way down, they'd already seen some mule deer, bighorn sheep and an eagle soaring above them. It was definitely a world away from the hectic pace of her life in Denver. She'd been telling herself for months that she needed to take some time off and come back here. There was more to life than just working, and standing here in the middle of God's creation today had reminded her why.

"I'm glad you talked me into this," she said, breathing in the fresh mountain air.

"Rough week?" Aaron asked.

"Rough month, actually, but one of my toughest cases is finally over, and now I'm just trying to forget it."

"What happened?" he asked. "You seem... I don't know. Tenser than normal."

"There were threats made by a defendant, but it's nothing I haven't faced before."

"Why didn't you tell me?"

"Because it's over."

At least she hoped it was.

She felt a shiver run down her spine despite the warm weather as she tried to push back the vivid memories. Carter Steele had caught her gaze in the courtroom, then slowly traced his finger across his throat. The implication had been clear, and she'd tried to shake the fear for days. But giving in to it wasn't an option. Instead, she'd reported the threat and was thankful that Steele had been convicted and locked away.

She took another sip of water, then shoved the bottle into the side pocket of her backpack. Threats against her were simply a hazard of being a prosecutor, and not something she could dwell on. Which was exactly why she'd needed this weekend to get away.

"You know you can always come to me if you're in trouble," Aaron said, interrupting her thoughts. "I've got more than a little experience with people like that."

"I'll be fine, Aaron. Really."

"Then here's what I want to know. Are you going to be able to make it back up to the top once we reach the bottom of the canyon?"

"Are you kidding me?" She shot her brother a grin. The off-the-beaten-trail trip down into the canyon might have been one of the toughest hikes she'd ever attempted because of the steep slope, but while it was a welcome challenge, it was also a chance to catch up with her brother. "Not only am I going to make it to the top, I'm going to beat you there. But first we need to keep going."

She grabbed her backpack and started back down the trail, knowing she'd pay for it physically over the next few days, but that was okay. For as long as she could remember, she and Aaron had been competitive about everything they did together. And, as the oldest, she'd always had a burning desire to win. That drive had begun to mellow over recent years, and while she still enjoyed their lively debates and friendly competition, fostering their relationship after the death of their parents was what she was really interested in. That and making sure she avoided the poison ivy and didn't slip off the edge of the steep trail.

They continued chatting about his last bounty-hunting job and her next case for another forty-five minutes, then he signaled her to stop at a relatively level section. She pulled out her water bottle again and adjusted the straps on her backpack, being extra careful this time to watch her feet on the loose gravel that made up the majority of the trail.

Her heart raced as something rustled in the trees. Seconds later, a falcon soared out from its perch above them.

"You really are jumpy today," Aaron said.

"I'm fine. I just thought I heard someone—or something—coming down the trail."

She glanced behind her, but there were no other hikers for as far as she could see. Which was what she liked about this portion of the canyon. It was possible to spend all day in this isolated part of the world and not run in to anyone.

She heard another noise, this time the distinct sound of falling gravel, and looked behind her again. The two masked men ran up behind them on the trail.

The taller man immediately grabbed her, pinning her arms behind her and throwing her off balance. Aaron lunged forward to stop him, but the second man pointed his gun at Aaron's head. Gwen's mind spun. While it rarely happened, she'd heard of hikers being robbed at gunpoint, or their cars being broken into while they were on the trail, but she never expected it to happen to her. Not here.

She screamed and tried to pull away from her captor, terrified he was going to shove her over the edge.

Instead, he pinned her tighter against him. "There's nobody around to hear you, so shut up."

"What do you want?" Gwen asked.

The older man took a step forward. "I'll make it simple—"

Without waiting for an explanation, Aaron lunged forward in an effort to disarm the man, but his plan backfired as both men slammed into Gwen. The man holding her lost his grip while Gwen lost her balance and slipped off the steep slope of the canyon.

Caden O'Callaghan heard a bloodcurdling scream and immediately tried to determine the direction of the source. It seemed to be coming from right above him. As a former army ranger, he was trained to run toward trouble—never away—and this was no exception. Because what he'd just heard could only mean one thing in this isolated spot—someone was in trouble. And out here, with resources limited, the consequences could be severe. His hand automatically rested on his Glock. Spending five days alone on the trail, the extra protection was a no-brainer for him. And while he hadn't had to use it so far, he'd always rather be prepared.

Seconds later, he caught sight of three men in a standoff on a slight ledge on the trail, with two masked men holding a gun on the third man. Caden pulled his weapon out of its holster and continued up the trail.

One of the armed men shifted his aim to his hostage's head and shouted at Caden. "Back off, or I will shoot him."

"Don't do it," Caden said. "Drop your weapons now."

Caden kept the barrel of his weapon trained on them as he evaluated the situation. Their hostage looked to be in his mid-twenties and had all the telltale signs of a military service member, judging from his short haircut and stance.

"They shoved my sister over the edge," their hostage yelled. "You've got to find her—"

"Shut up." One of the men gripped his arm tighter as they started backing away, keeping him in front of them. "Stay out of this."

Caden held his weapon steady, unwilling to withdraw. "Sorry. I'm already involved, and I said drop your weapons."

"Back. Off. Now. I will shoot him."

Caden hesitated, then lowered his gun to his side, unwilling to risk the man following through with his threat.

"Don't follow us."

The two men continued to edge their way up the trail, forcing the hostage with them. Ten, fifteen… twenty feet… Caden weighed his options. He could go after the men, but if the sister really had fallen over the edge, she needed to be his priority.

He watched as the three men disappeared around the bend, then immediately moved to where there were scuff marks off the side of the trail…but no sign of the woman. He pulled out his cell, hoping to call for help, then frowned when there was no signal. He was going to have to do this on his own.

Caden pulled a pair of binoculars from his back-pack, then studied the terrain below that was sprinkled with trees and brush. He followed the trajectory of where the woman would have fallen, but still couldn't see any signs of anyone. Which had him worried. Unless something had stopped her fall, there was no way to know how far she'd dropped. And on top of that, in order to find her, he was going to have to veer off the trail. Depending on where she'd landed, the chance of her surviving a fall without injury was slim.

"Hello?"

He stood still for a moment, waiting for a response, but there was nothing.

The steep, unmaintained trails leading down to the base of the canyon were known for their difficulty, and there were even warnings posted to visitors regarding the dangers. The sun wouldn't set for a few more hours, but because of the steep, narrow walls, shadows had already begun to fall across the bottom of the canyon. Even with his climbing skills, the descent was going to be difficult.

He started down the incline, careful to secure his footing with each step, while trying to avoid the poison ivy snaking across the slope. While deaths here were relatively rare, they did happen, typically from either falling off the steep walls of the canyon or rafting-related accidents in the water below. Most of the time tragedy struck because of people's unpreparedness. Sometimes, it was simply being in the wrong place at the wrong time.

His feet skidded on a patch of loose dirt, and he grabbed a branch to stop himself from sliding any farther. So much for his quiet few days of solo backpacking in God's wilderness. He continued on, moving as fast as possible while still being careful. These off-trails were marked as self-rescue, meaning if you did get hurt, you couldn't rely on the authorities to help you out. Once he reached the missing woman, he'd have to figure out how to get her the help she needed on his own.

Thirty feet down, he found a red backpack that had gotten snagged on some brush. He stared ahead of him. It had to be hers. But where was she? Another five hundred feet below him, the river roared through the narrow canyon bottom. If she'd fallen that far, there was no way she would have survived.

A flash of movement caught his attention. He zoomed in on the site with his binoculars and found her, wedged between the slope and a shrub tree. His heart raced as he scrambled down the last twenty feet to where he'd spotted the woman and tried not to push any of the loose rocks down on her in the process. He'd seen movement—which implied she was alive—but depending on how badly she was injured, he still had to figure out how to get her out of this canyon.

She was lying on her side when he got there, blood running down her forehead where she must have hit it on something. There were scratches across her arms and a long gash on her right calf. He watched her chest rise and fall and let out an audible gasp of relief. A foot or two to the right and she could easily have ended up at the bottom of the canyon.

He crouched down beside her, surprised at how familiar she looked. He searched his memory for a name, but came up with nothing.

"Ma'am…" He gently grasped her shoulder. "Ma'am, I'm here to help."

She groaned as she tried to turn toward him.

"Hold on…" he said, recognition still playing in the back of his mind. "I need you to stay still until I can determine where you're injured."

He unzipped his backpack and pulled out a bandana and his water bottle. After soaking the cloth in the water, he started wiping the blood off her forehead. There was a cut along her temple that probably needed stiches, but it didn't look too serious.

Her eyes widened as she looked up at him. "Caden?"

He pulled back his hand and stared at her a few more seconds as the realization hit him like a punch to the gut.

"Gwen?"

Of course. Gwen Ryland. How could he forget the woman who'd accused him of breaking her best friend's heart? A flood of memories surfaced, but none of that mattered at the moment. Still, he couldn't help but wonder how he'd managed to run into the one woman in the entire state who hated him.

But what she thought about him didn't matter at the moment.

"How did you find me?" she asked.

"I was out hiking the falls today." He hesitated. She had to have seen the two men that had taken her brother, but he wasn't sure how much she knew.

She pressed her hand against her head, as if trying to remember what had happened. "Where's my brother? They grabbed him. Had a gun on him."

"They took him up the hill. There was nothing I could

do to stop them, but he told me you'd slid off the trail. You became the priority."

"I need to find him." She managed to sit up.

"Slow down." Caden pressed his hands against her shoulders. "We'll figure out where he is, but you're not going anywhere right now. I need to know where you're hurt."

She frowned. "It might be easier to tell you where I'm not hurt, but my left shoulder is throbbing pretty badly."

Caden started carefully checking her over. "It doesn't look like it's fractured, though I can't be 100 percent sure until it's x-rayed. Do you think you can walk down the rest of the way if I help you?"

"Do I have a choice?" She winced as she tried to stand up.

"Does your ankle hurt? It looks a little swollen."

"It feels sprained. But only mildly. I think I can walk." She put pressure on it, winced again, then took a step. "What I need to do is find my brother, and if they took him up the trail—"

"You'll never make it back up the trail like this—"

"I have to find him."

He heard the sharpness in her voice and bit back his frustration. He might have purposely buried memories of her and Cammie all these years, but he did remember how stubborn she'd been. Clearly nothing had changed. But she was right. Her brother's life was in danger, but his wasn't the only one. Finding her had only been the first step. He had to get her out of this canyon.

"Let's take one thing at a time. Even if there were enough hours of daylight left, there's no way you can walk back up before it gets dark. But if I get you down to the bottom of the canyon, I've got a camp set up not far upstream with a first-aid kit."

"And my brother?"

"We'll search for phone service and try to get help."

She frowned, but he knew he was right. Traversing the trail was difficult enough for a fit person, which meant it was still going to take them two or three times as long to reach the bottom of the canyon with her injuries. On top of that, even if they could get a hold of the authorities, it might take hours for help to arrive. Their best plan was to get her down to his camp and clean her up the best he could, then try to find help in the morning.

"Do you have any idea why they targeted you?" he asked.

"I don't know. It all happened so fast."

"Did you get a look at their faces?"

She shook her head. "No."

"Me, neither."

"I'm pretty sure they weren't expecting any witnesses to whatever their plan was," she said.

"What about enemies?" he asked.

"It's possible." He didn't miss the hesitation in her voice. "I'm a prosecutor, so I've faced my share of run-ins with bad guys, but this... I don't know."

He'd press for answers later. Right now, he needed to get her off the canyon wall and somewhere safer.

"Stay behind me and be careful. The actual trail is difficult enough since it's not maintained, but this is going to be even rougher until we can get back to the trail."

Caden let out a sharp huff as he stared down the steep terrain toward the trail. Gravel slid beneath her feet behind him. He reached and grabbed her hand, then immediately caught the look of irritation in her eyes. Still, he held on to her a few more seconds to ensure she was okay.

"Thanks," she said.

He would have laughed if he didn't know how serious the circumstances were. He was certain that if he was the last person on the planet and she was in trouble, she still wouldn't want to accept his help. And that was fine. In truth, he didn't blame her. She only knew one side of the story, but at the time he knew it wouldn't have mattered what he said. Maybe he'd handled the situation wrong back then, but he knew the truth, and for him that was all that had mattered. And, in the end, he'd never regretted his decision to walk away. He'd never looked back.

"You remember who I am, don't you?" she asked.

"Of course." He needed to find a way to cut the tension between them. "You haven't changed at all."

It was true. After ten years, her blue eyes were just as intense, and her hair, while a few inches shorter, had the same honey-blond highlights.

"Do you still live near here?" she said.

"I work on my father's ranch."

He paused, wanting to ignore the questions he knew were hanging between them. Questions she had to assume he was going to ask.

How is Camille? Has she gone on with her life?

But they were questions he had no desire to pose. Instead, he decided to shift the conversation back to her.

"Are you—?"

He didn't get a chance to finish as a shot rang out and a bullet slammed into the tree beside them.

TWO

There was no time to react. The realization they were being shot at had just barely registered in Gwen's mind when Caden grabbed her hand and pulled her behind the trunk of a spindly tree for cover. A second shot rang out, this time hitting the bark above them.

He signaled at her to stay down, then fired two shots in the direction of the shooter before ducking back behind the tree beside her. "We need to keep going."

She nodded, then followed him down the steep incline. Her mind spun as it tried to process everything that had happened. The men grabbing them. Slipping off the trail and tumbling down the side of the canyon. Realizing whoever had just shot at them also had her brother. It was like a nightmare she couldn't wake up from.

But he was right. With at least one shooter after them, they couldn't stop now.

Adrenaline masked most of the pain as she followed his lead. All it would take was one slight misstep, and she could slip again. And this time, there might not be anything to stop her fall.

"You can't hide out here," the man shouted from above them, rustling through the brush as he made his way closer. "I will find you."

Caden pulled her into a small, hollowed-out depression just big enough for the two of them and signaled for her to be quiet.

Heart pounding, she listened for movement. A small avalanche of stones trickled over the lip of the hollowed-out area above them. Her mouth went dry. The shooter was there, somewhere above them. Looking. Searching. She could hear rustling in the brush. Another small shower of rocks.

Then suddenly everything was silent. She waited, holding her breath until her lungs began to burn, then slowly let out the air.

Where was he?

"Do you think he's gone?" she whispered.

"It sounded like he headed back toward the trail."

She glanced up at the sunlight drenching the top of the canyon, but where they were, shadows had already begun to move in. Before long, it would be dark, and the terrain would be too dangerous to navigate. A bird called out, echoing below them, as every unfamiliar sound around them sent her heart racing. She tried to shake off the layer of fear that had settled over her, but it was impossible.

"Do you think you can keep going?" he asked. "We can still take it slow, but I don't want to make this descent after dark, and we'll quickly run out of daylight if we don't start moving."

She nodded, determined to keep up with him despite the pain. She started down beside him in silence, ignoring the sounds around them that echoed off the canyon walls, focusing instead on each step. And she listened for any signs that the shooter was still out there. But with every minute that passed, there was nothing to indicate they were being followed.

Then where were they? Had the men given up? Were they planning to use her brother as leverage to get to her? There was no way to know the men's endgame. All she could do now was make it to the bottom of the canyon, then find a way out of here alive.

By the time they got to Caden's camp, she was exhausted and hurting. A one-man tent had been set up on the edge of a small clearing a few dozen feet from the nearby river. Canyon walls surrounded them, reaching toward the cloudy spring sky that was already chasing away the last bits of light. It was the untamed wilderness, with its scattering of scrub oak, sagebrush and aspen, that made it a favorite for people wanting to escape the modern world for a short time. And that was the reason she'd chosen to come here.

"This is a beautiful spot," she said.

"I camp here every year. Spend a few days hiking by myself. Gives me some time to reevaluate things." He helped her sit down on a sleeping mat. "I'll go grab my first-aid kit."

As she watched him head inside the tent, she struggled to pinpoint what was different about him from the last time she'd seen him. He was still quiet and serious, and he looked the same with his brown hair, blue-gray eyes and tall, muscular frame. Even she couldn't deny the appeal of his rugged stature, with his cowboy hat and the start of a beard. But that wasn't what had changed. Instead, he seemed more…calm. Focused. Not that it really mattered. She'd seen him walk out on Cammie, and while she was grateful he'd saved her life, she'd never fall for a guy she couldn't trust not to do the same to her.

He came back out with the small kit and opened it. "You're going to need some painkillers. There should also be some antiseptic wipes in here for any cuts, and I've got clean water if you're out."

"I should have some water in my backpack, as well as some food."

The last thing she wanted was to make him think she expected him to take care of her out here. She'd come prepared for anything. Well…almost anything.

"Good, then we should have plenty to last us through tomorrow." He nodded at her backpack. "Go ahead and drink some more water. We need to stay hydrated."

She followed his instructions and took a long swig, while he pulled out what they needed. The same awkwardness that had followed them down the canyon settled in between them again. They'd been silent most of the way down, and when they had spoken to each other, they'd never gotten beyond the basic small talk. Which, in all honestly, had been fine with her.

"How long were you planning to stay out here?" Caden asked.

"We were just going to hike down and back up in one day."

Caden, on the other hand, was clearly prepared for a week out in the wilderness.

"I can rig a splint for your ankle, but that and the

pain medicine is really all we can do at this point, other than clean you up," he said.

"I don't think I need a splint, but I will take the pain medicine." She grabbed the two pills he offered her and popped them into her mouth.

He pulled out an antiseptic pad and quickly cleaned up the smaller scrapes on her forehead and arms, then grabbed a second one for the larger cut on her calf.

"Do you think it needs stitches?" she asked.

"I don't think so. It will leave a scar, but you should be okay."

"Where'd you get your medical training?"

"After college I joined the army."

His answer didn't surprise her. She remembered he'd been organized and efficient when she'd known him in college, along with a number of other things she'd rather forget. But she wasn't too stubborn to recognize the fact that she needed him.

Her jaw tightened as he cleaned the gash. "Thank you. For rescuing me."

"It's not over yet, but by this time tomorrow we should be out of here, in touch with the authorities and hopefully have found your brother."

"I'm worried about him," she said.

"I know. We'll find him." Caden took another couple of minutes to finish, then stood up. "I want you to lie down and keep your foot elevated while I get some dinner going."

"Wait…there's something you need to know first," she said.

"Okay." He sat back down and caught her gaze. "What's that?"

She hesitated to bring up the matter that had been plaguing her since the attack, but he needed to know. "I don't think this was random."

"Did you know those men?"

"No, but I think I know who sent them."

"Who?"

She drew in a deep breath. "I believe it's connected with my job."

"As a prosecutor?"

She nodded. "His name is Carter Steele. He was arrested for domestic abuse, drug trafficking and child endangerment. I reported the threat he made toward me in the courtroom, but didn't think he could actually follow through. Not from prison. But this... I can't just dismiss this as a coincidence. Which also means I'm sorry for the entire situation I just roped you into."

"It wasn't your fault."

"Maybe not, but you've still been dragged into it. Threats like this have increased over the past few years, and while most won't follow through, this... I think this has to be related."

"You think he wants you dead?"

"Whoever was out there shot at us, so it seems likely. What I don't understand is why didn't they just break into my apartment or run me off the road on the highway. This whole setup was extremely dangerous."

"It was, but it also makes sense on one level," Caden said. "An accident here would be easy to cover up. A couple of hikers fall off the rim, bodies are found a few days or months later, or not at all. Everyone would simply believe it was an accident."

She felt a shudder run through her. If that had been their plan, and she was still alive…

"So they grabbed my brother…for what? To use as leverage?"

"Maybe, and then they came after you because they need to make sure you're dead."

"If that's what they want, then we have to assume they'll be back."

Caden nodded. "Which means we need to be ready."

Twenty minutes later, Caden dumped the dry pasta into the boiling water on top of his small propane stove. So much for his five days of solitude in the mountains. He worked to rein in his irritation over the entire situation. It wasn't that he minded helping out a fellow hiker—it was simply that he'd managed to run into *her*. But feeding his irritation was only going to make him even more agitated, and there was no reason to let her control how he felt.

He flicked a fly off his pant leg and frowned. Had he let Cammie's betrayal affect him so much that he'd managed to shut himself off from feeling or caring for anyone again? He loved working on the ranch, because it made him feel free. He didn't have to concern himself with anyone else. Just him and the open range. But what if he really wasn't as free as he thought he was? What if he was still running because of Cammie?

He glanced at Gwen's profile. While he hadn't known her well, they had hung out a few times with his fiancée and several of their other friends. Until the night Cammie had called off their wedding and walked out on him, blaming the break up on him.

At the time, he hadn't even seen it coming, and Cammie had caught him completely off guard. Though, looking back, all the signs had been there. Unfortunately, he'd been young, and somehow thought Cammie's devotion to their relationship had been as strong as his. That had proven to be just one of many lies Cammie had told him.

But for now, none of that mattered. He'd formulated a plan. While the distance to the top of the canyon was just over a mile, the vertical drop was so steep, experts estimated it took double or even triple the descent time when going back up. He'd noted how long it had taken them to make it to the bottom. Going up would be even slower for her, if not impossible. The only alternate route was the river, but even that came with its own set of issues. The shoreline was often narrow and bordered with slippery rocks. Rafters frequently tackled the challenge, but there were sections that should only be attempted by those with experience. More than one overconfident person had lost his life from a foolish move on the water. But Caden believed she'd be able to handle the water route better than trying to hike back up the canyon.

Gwen walked toward him across the small campsite as he was adjusting the propane bottle, then sat down on one of the logs across from him.

"How are you feeling?" Caden asked, not missing the frown on her face.

"Sore, but thankfully the pain medicine is finally starting to kick in."

"Good." He bent down and looked at her ankle. "It's still a bit swollen, but that's expected considering you just walked down the canyon on an injured ankle. You still need to keep it elevated, but it should be better by tomorrow."

"I know I should be lying down, but I just felt so restless," she said. "I was wondering if you had a plan?"

His hand automatically touched the butt of his weapon. "Until morning, we're going to have to keep our guard up. Then I'm hoping we can find a group of rafters to join so we can head downriver. That would be the easiest way out for you."

"But still dangerous."

He nodded.

"What about my brother?"

"He's another reason we need to get out of here as soon as possible, so we can let the authorities know what's going on. Even if I wasn't worried about your ankle, we can't go after your brother in the dark."

"I know, I just—I just need to do something." She picked up a small stick and snapped it in two. "Tell me what I can do to help with dinner in the meantime."

"Well, I wasn't planning on company, but pasta alfredo with salmon was on the menu for tonight." He'd already grabbed the ingredients for the meal that had been neatly packed in a plastic Ziploc in his bear-resistant canister. "I don't think it will be a stretch to feed two."

"Pasta alfredo with smoked salmon?" she asked.

He hesitated. "You don't like salmon?"

"No… I mean, yes. Salmon's fine, but is this how you always eat on the trail? That sounds like a gourmet meal."

"What did you expect?"

"I don't know—ramen noodles and a packet of tuna fish."

He chuckled. "I like to cook and realized years ago that just because I'm not standing in the middle of my kitchen doesn't mean I can't eat well on the trail. Tonight's pasta, but I can also make a mean chili from sun-dried tomatoes and dehydrated kidney beans."

She shot him an unexpected smile. "All I can say is I'm impressed."

He shoved off the compliment and started organizing the food. He'd also learned early on that an hour or two of food prep before he hit the trail translated into a much more enjoyable trip. And as long as the food was light and quick to fix—meaning no cooking, just boiled water—it wasn't that difficult to carry.

He handed her a small bunch of fresh basil from his mother's garden along with a knife. "If you'll mince this, I'll get the pasta going. Then we'll just have to add the ingredients for the sauce I already put together back at the house."

"Of course you did."

This time he wasn't sure if she was being sarcastic or complimentary, but she was smiling, so he decided to go with the latter. He dumped the pasta into the water, and for a moment, working beside her seemed oddly...normal. While he loved the solitude of the trail and a solo hike, there were times when he missed the sound of another human's voice. If only he could forget not only that someone was after them, but also who *she* was, he might actually enjoy tonight.

A noise behind them seized his attention.

He took a step back from the stove and shifted his concentration to the shadows filtering down the canyon wall. He scanned the surrounding vegetation, senses on alert, but the movement was just a squirrel. He let out a huff of air.

"What if they come back?" she asked.

"I've already thought about that."

"And?"

"While you were lying down, I rigged a trip wire around the camp."

"An alarm in case they find us?"

Caden nodded.

"How'd you do that?"

"Fishing wire and key-chain alarm. It's pretty rudimentary, but it should do the trick if they show up." He stirred the pasta, then tested it to see if it was done. "I don't usually set one, but I'd say we have reason tonight."

"I agree."

"I also don't want either of us sleeping in the tent. If they show up, that's where they're going to assume we are."

She nodded as they worked side by side for the next few minutes, mixing the dry sauce ingredients with water and letting it simmer, then combining it with the pasta, freeze-dried corn, smoked salmon and the fresh basil.

"This is delicious," she said, once they'd dished up the food.

"You look surprised."

"Most guys I know could never pull this off."

"My mother ensured all of us boys knew our way around the kitchen."

"Well, I'm impressed." She took another bite. "I remember you had brothers. Three of them, right?"

Caden nodded.

"What do they do now?" she asked.

"Reid works for the local fire department in Timber Falls. Liam is in the army and is married with a daughter and has another one on the way."

"That's exciting. And number three?"

"Griffin is a deputy and getting married in December."

"And you—you left the military?"

"My father had a bout with cancer a couple years ago, and while he's made a full recovery, I was at a place in my career that I felt like it was time to walk away and help. I've been running the ranch with him ever since."

"I remember you talking about your ranch when we were in school. It always sounded so beautiful."

"It is."

"Do you ever regret your decision?"

He shifted in his seat, uncomfortable with all her personal questions. "There are things I miss about the military, but I love working on the land every day. I just decided if I was going to do it, I wouldn't look back."

"Still, that had to be hard."

"It was. And to be honest, it still is sometimes, but I love what I do." He stood and headed for his bear barrel, needing a distraction from her questions. "How about some chocolate cookie bars?"

"Why am I not surprised? That would top off a perfect meal."

He grabbed two, then handed her one. "You said you're a prosecutor. What kind of cases do you work on?"

"I focus primarily on family law."

"Do you like it?"

"I do, though the cases can be tough. I represent children most of the time."

"I bet you're good at it."

"It has its rewarding moments."

He took a bite of his cookie and frowned. He hadn't planned on giving her a compliment, even though he'd meant it. But smoked-salmon pasta and chocolate couldn't make him forget whom he was sitting next to.

"I guess you heard Cammie got married," she said without warning.

He set down his dessert and frowned at the news. For a moment, he could have almost imagined that they were simply old friends catching up. But now, hearing his ex-fiancée's name made him want to run.

"I did," he said finally. "Do you ever see her?"

"We used to get together several times a year, but they moved to Dallas, and I haven't seen her as much since then."

"Is she happy?"

He frowned, wondering why he'd asked the question. Why it even mattered after all this time. She was a part of his past, and he was content to leave her there.

"She seems happy. Rick's a decent guy."

The unspoken tension hung between them. He knew what Gwen was thinking. Knew she'd probably never forgiven him for what she thought he'd done. She'd made it clear that night exactly what she thought about him, and he hadn't tried to convince her otherwise. At the time, it didn't seem to matter. He'd known the truth wasn't going to change anything. Cammie would have walked away no matter what he said.

"So you never married?" he asked.

She glanced at her left hand. "I came close once, but in the end our goals ended up being too different. I guess I was looking for something more."

He thought he'd found that something more with Cammie. He knew her friends had blamed him for the breakup the night before their wedding, but he'd decided that was fine with him. He knew the truth, and in the end, that was all that really mattered.

As far as he was concerned, he was okay with being the bad guy in the whole scenario. He'd gone on with his life, and while he still might not be able to trust his judgment when it came to picking women, at least he could live with his conscience.

He caught the fatigue in her eyes as she yawned beside him. "Why don't you try to get some sleep. I'll stay up."

"You can't stay awake all night."

"It wouldn't be the first time." He could tell she wanted to argue with him, but he didn't miss the exhaustion in her eyes. "I'll be fine."

"Wake me up in a few hours and I'll keep watch. You're going to need your rest just as much as me."

Twenty minutes later, she was asleep, and he was going through his gear, needing to be prepared to run if the men showed up. If he'd been on his own, he would have approached the situation differently, but he wasn't looking for another confrontation against armed men with Gwen's safety at stake.

He finished packing a go bag, then pulled out his Bible. He settled in on his camping chair, aware of the night noises around him as he stared up at the sliver of stars above him, and started praying that he'd be able to get her out of here before the men found them. Praying that Gwen wouldn't get under his skin. He didn't even know he'd fallen asleep until the blare of his trip wire going off jolted him awake.

THREE

Gwen heard the screech of an alarm go off, then quickly fought to dig herself out of the dream and orient herself. A couple seconds later, Caden was hovering over her.

"They found us. We have to leave. Now."

He grabbed her hand and helped her up, as everything rushed through her in one terrifying flash of memory. She could hear the men yelling at each other in the middle of the camp as they ran toward the tent, shouting her name. There was no doubt they were looking for her. No doubt Caden's plan had bought them the extra seconds they needed to escape.

She stumbled to her feet beside him, thankful not only for his suggestion to sleep in her shoes, but also for the full moon high above them. The problem was, even with the moon out, there was still barely enough light to see where they were going because of the tree cover. Pain shot up her calf as she rushed through the brush with him, but she refused to let it slow her down. She knew how this could play out if they didn't run. Those men were armed, and from everything she knew, they planned to kill her when they found her.

Caden kept his arm around her, steadying her on the rugged path as the voices in the camp faded.

"What time is it?" she whispered.

"Just past two."

"Where are we going?" she asked.

"There's a shallow spot in the river nearby. We need to cross over, then head downstream on the other side. After I set the trip wire, I left a trail of false tracks heading upstream. Hopefully they'll follow them and buy us more time."

And then what? She knew she couldn't keep running. Not for long. She glanced up at his profile as he tightened his arm around her. As much as she didn't like it, Caden O'Callaghan held her life in his hands, and she was going to have to trust him.

She struggled to catch her breath as he led her into the icy river water. She'd known that he'd planned on trying to catch a ride down the river in the morning, but there was one thing she hadn't mentioned. Her fear of water. Panic swallowed her. She gripped his hand harder but wasn't going to let him see the fear. The water was shallow here, like he'd told her, but it still rushed across her calves, almost to her knees. She took another step, and another, fear of the men behind her compelling her forward.

At the middle point of the river, she glanced back toward the camp. Beams of light hit the tree line. The men were still rummaging for clues as to where they'd gone. Confirmation they were at the right place. But it wouldn't be long before they extended the perimeter of their search. Her foot slipped on a rock—she couldn't allow herself to be dragged into the water. All it would take was one misstep, and she'd end up sucked into the current.

But Caden was there to steady her.

"Gwen?"

"I'm fine."

"How are you really feeling?"

She hesitated. "Like I was hit by a truck."

"I'm not surprised," he said as they kept walking. "What about your head?"

"Just a slight headache."

"As soon as we can stop, I'll get you some more pain medicine. Any nausea or dizziness?"

She was shaking now, as much from the cold as from fear. "I'm just sore and tired."

She knew what he was thinking. Headache, confusion, dizziness, nausea—the symptoms of a concussion. If it was a concussion, treatment meant she needed to rest, but there was no more time for that. Instead, they were looking at a long hike out of here. Her only option was to push through.

They stepped onto the other bank and started downstream, keeping to the dark shadows of the canyon to ensure they stayed hidden.

"I'll be fine."

They walked in silence along the side of the river. She tried not to think about where her brother was, or what would happen if the men found them. She just had to keep moving. Had to make sure the men didn't catch up to them. Caden stopped every twenty yards or so and listened to the night sounds. She could no longer see the flashlights or hear the people after her, but she knew they were out there.

"Did you hear something?" she asked.

"Yes, I'm just not sure if it's them."

Another few yards down the river, he steered them behind an outcropping of trees. She was barely able to distinguish his movements as Caden pulled his weapon out of his holster. Gwen shivered in the darkness. She had no idea what their plan should be, or how they were going to defend themselves if those men struck again. But clearly, they needed to be ready for anything.

"Caden…"

"Have you ever used a gun?" he asked.

"A few times at a shooting range. Why?"

"I need to go out there and figure out which way they've gone. Make sure they're not behind us, but I don't want to risk doing that with you. I also can't leave you defenseless."

She shook her head, wanting to scream at him not to leave her, but she knew he was right. They needed to know where the men were. But was leaving her alone the solution?

"You'll be fine if you stay here." He tilted back her chin and caught her gaze. "I promise I'll be back."

"I don't want the gun. You'll be defenseless."

"I have no plans to confront them. Not at this point, anyway."

He rechecked the weapon. "Leave the safety on and don't shoot unless you absolutely have to. And when I come back…don't shoot me."

She watched him walk away, then stood frozen in

the shadows until she lost track of time. Five, ten… fifteen minutes… She had no idea how much time had passed, but she heard every sound around her. Her ankle throbbed and her head pounded. She didn't want to be here alone and hated the helpless feeling overtaking her. Hated that she was a liability. But there was nothing she could do to change the situation.

She studied the surrounding terrain, listening carefully for anything that sounded out of place, but every noise caused her pulse to quicken and her heart to race. What if something had happened to Caden? What if she was left alone to find her way out of the canyon? The river churned beside her, crickets chirped. If those men were out there, close by… No. She gripped the gun tighter. She wasn't going to panic. She had to be ready. Caden was counting on her to stay calm. Which made her want to laugh. As part of her job, she'd stood her ground to protect dozens of vulnerable children who had dealt with domestic violence, trauma and child abuse, but put her in the middle of a potential gunfight and her only instinct was to run.

Something rustled behind her.

She turned around and aimed the weapon in front of her. "Whoever you are, don't come any closer. I'm armed."

"Gwen…it's just me."

Her heart pounded as Caden came into view. She took a step backward and realized she'd been holding her breath. "Are you okay?"

"I'm fine."

She handed him the gun, barrel first, glad to have the weapon out of her hands. "Did you find them?"

"They're headed upstream like I hoped. Can you keep moving?"

She nodded.

"Good, because we need to put as much distance between us and them as possible. And in the meantime, pray we find someone to take us downriver once the sun comes up."

Caden glanced at her, impressed by the grit and determination in her step, knowing it had to be painful. Not that it changed anything. She'd once told him exactly what she thought about him, and he was pretty sure that even with all the time that had passed, her feelings toward him hadn't changed, either.

He'd never been able to forget her words that night. She'd caught up with him in the parking lot as he was leaving the rehearsal dinner. Twenty-four hours before he was supposed to marry Cammie. Instead, everything he'd thought was real—everything he'd believed about his fiancée—had all turned out to be a lie, and his plans for the future had suddenly come crumbling down around him.

If you don't think she's the one you want to spend the rest of your life with, then fine. Better now than after you're married. But I hope you never forget what your selfishness is about to cost you.

He'd stood in front of Gwen, lights from the barn where they'd planned the dinner twinkling in the background. He'd wanted to tell her the truth. That his actions hadn't been what broke things off between him and Cammie. But he'd seen the anger in Gwen's eyes and knew how loyal she was to her friend. No matter what he would have said at that moment, she never would have believed him. And all these years later, he was sure she still wouldn't.

Gwen let out a soft groan next to him.

He grabbed her waist to make sure she didn't fall. "Gwen…"

"Sorry, I just stepped wrong. I'm fine."

He studied her gait. Her limp was definitely more pronounced.

"You're not fine. We need to stop." He flipped on his flashlight, then reached down and checked her ankle. "It's swelling again."

"I'm fine, Caden. I can keep going."

"If you don't take care of this, you won't be able to walk out of here. We've put some distance between them and us. You need to take some pain medicine, soak your ankle in the river water and rest, at least for a few minutes."

She hesitated, then nodded. "Fine. But just for a few minutes."

"We'll leave your shoe on in case your ankle starts swelling."

He found a small inlet, where the water moved slower next to the shoreline and there was an outcropping of rocks where they could sit. He handed her the pain medicine and some water from his backpack, then kneeled down in front of her and eased her shoe into the water. It might not be an ice pack, but it was the next best thing.

"How does that feel?" he asked.

"Cold, but good."

Moonlight filtered down the canyon wall, bathing the rock's crevices in a soft glow of light before shifting across the water. While he loved exploring the canyon during the day, there had always been something captivating about the scene at night.

"You're shaking," he said, sitting down beside her. He needed to get her out of here.

"I'm just cold."

"The temperatures drop significantly down here at night." He moved closer to her and wrapped his arm around her. "On the bright side, it gets too cold for venomous snakes."

She shivered next to him. "I've tried not to think about what might be out here."

He glanced across the darkened river, knowing it was impossible. The most dangerous enemy out there wasn't the wildlife.

She needed a distraction.

"I'd like to hear more about your job," he said. "You mentioned you represent children."

"Yeah. The center I work for was started to help ensure that child victims didn't fall through the cracks. We work primarily through stopping any abuse before it starts, but we also support victims of all forms of abuse."

"Sounds like an important mission."

"It is. We end up being advocates for these families through the entire process, giving counsel and support through the criminal investigation and ensuring that the victims and their families have the resources they need."

"That's got to be a challenge."

"It is. While I love my job, I want to do more than

the system allows. One of our goals is preventing abuse but there are still issues that are hard to deal with."

"Meaning?"

"I help ensure the children get placed into a safe environment and defend their rights, but most of these kids need more than that. They need help learning how to communicate and resolve conflicts. And also figuring out what they are made of. That with the right resources they can thrive."

"Any ideas on how to do that?"

"Yes, actually. I've spent the past few months researching several programs for at-risk teens that are located right here in the state. So many kids struggle navigating into adulthood, but the potential is there. If they aren't intentionally worked with, most of them will never reach that potential. And the majority of the kids I deal with don't have anyone at home to advocate for them, let alone teach them basic life skills. All they need sometimes is someone who cares. Someone who can teach them how to problem-solve and set goals. I've seen it work firsthand, but instead, we're losing too many of our young people."

"You're passionate about these kids."

"Sorry." She let out a low laugh. "I do tend to go overboard when someone asks me."

"You have nothing to be sorry about. Anyone can go to work every day and do their job, but I find so many people end up losing the passion that put them there in the first place. Sounds like you haven't done that."

"One of the things I'm actually looking at is a wilderness program where at-risk youths, in particular, can address issues and uncover their strengths in an outdoor setting."

"Maybe I'm wrong, but I don't remember you being the outdoor type."

She shook her head. "I wasn't. Not back in college, at least. I was definitely more of a bookworm."

"What changed?"

She hesitated, making him wonder if he'd asked the wrong question.

"Aaron and I... Our parents were killed in a car crash about six years ago by a drunk driver," she said, finally.

"Wow... I'm so sorry."

"It turned our world on end, but especially for my brother. He was nineteen, impulsive and anything but serious about life. I struggled reaching him for a long time, but eventually found that this was a way for us to connect. He loves the outdoors, so we plan something different every few months. We've hiked Pikes Peak, the Rio Grande Trail, Bear Creek Falls... Last year we even tried downhill mountain-biking for the first time at Crested Butte."

"He's fortunate to have you."

"It's mutual. Losing someone you love changes you. It makes you realize how fragile life is and reminds you not to take people for granted." She pulled her foot out of the water. "We should go. They know I'm injured, and more than likely assume we're still around here. It's not going to take them too long to realize they're headed in the wrong direction."

He helped her up, knowing she was right. He hoped to have them both out of the canyon by dinnertime tomorrow, but there was no way to know how this would play out. Expecting to outrun the men if they came back was foolish. Which meant they were going to have to outsmart them, and the way to do that was to get out of here as soon as possible.

But he was already questioning his decision to try to leave via the water. There were too many sections that even experts found intimidating, and he wasn't sure if she'd be able to handle it physically. He shoved aside the questions. Worrying wasn't going to help and certainly wasn't going to change the situation. Once he got a signal on his cell, he could arrange for a helicopter to pick them up downriver, but in order to do that, they had to keep moving.

FOUR

The sun's rays crept along the canyon walls as Gwen stopped to drink a few sips of water. She estimated that they'd made it a mile downstream in the predawn light, but she knew she was slowing down Caden. The cold river water—along with the medicine he'd given her—had helped block the pain in her ankle, but the remaining aches still seemed minimal compared to the danger they were in. While there hadn't been any sign of the men after them, she knew it was just a matter of time. They *were* out there. Somewhere.

Maybe she was simply being paranoid, but on the other hand, she knew they had reason to worry. She'd tried praying as she drifted off to sleep—knowing how important sleep was—but she hadn't been able to get her mind to relax. Instead, she felt as if she'd spent most of the night running from masked giants in her dreams. And the men catching them wasn't her only fear. They'd taken her brother, and as tough as he was, he'd been unarmed and outnumbered.

All because of her.

"Do you need something to eat?" Caden asked, grabbing a protein bar out of his backpack.

"Thanks, but I've got some protein snacks." She pulled a blue package out of the side pocket of her backpack.

"What is that?"

She held up the package. "Chickpeas."

"Chickpeas?"

"Want to try them?"

Caden shook his head. "Thanks, but I think I'll pass."

She just smiled. "Your loss. All-natural, roasted and taste better—in my opinion—than peanuts."

For a moment she could almost forget this was the same man who'd broken her best friend's heart. He was good-looking and charming, and on top of that had rescued her. And yet she knew the truth about who he really was.

Caden stopped in front of her and pulled out his binoculars.

"What it is?" She scanned the river upstream, then saw a white raft headed toward them through the rapids.

"I think I just found our ticket out of here."

"You're sure it's not the guys after us?"

"Definitely not. One's bearded and the other's too dark."

Caden dropped his pack, then edged closer to the river and started waving his arms.

"You guys okay?" one of them shouted as they maneuvered the raft toward the shoreline.

"We could really use a ride out of here. She fell down the side of the canyon yesterday afternoon and is pretty banged up."

The bearded man grabbed a rope, then jumped onto the shore, securing the raft. "It might be a bit crowded, but we'll make it work."

Caden pulled the raft into the shallow water, then handed one of the men his backpack.

"Bruce McCleary." The taller one with the beard shook Caden's hand. "And this is Levi Wells. We're firefighters up in Wyoming, but try to get down here and make this run every year or two."

"I'm Caden O'Callaghan and this is Gwen Ryland." Caden glanced at her for a brief moment before turning back to the men. "There is something else you need to know."

"Like why you're carrying?" Bruce asked.

"I usually do while hiking solo as a precaution, but there are two armed men who attacked Gwen and her brother up on the trail. That's when she fell. They grabbed her brother, but they're still after her. We need to get somewhere where we can call the authorities."

"That sounds pretty personal," Levi said. "We won't get phone coverage for at least three or four miles downriver. On top of that, it's going to be a rough ride, but we should be able to get you there in one piece."

"So you're in?" Caden asked.

"Are you kidding?" Levi glanced at his friend and nodded. "Trouble never scared either of us away."

"We appreciate it," Gwen said.

Still, she hesitated at the bank. It wasn't as if things could get any worse. Or could they? She swallowed hard. No, they'd get on the raft, call for help and find her brother, then all of this would be over.

"You okay?" Caden asked.

"Yeah, I'm just…" She forced herself to step into the back of the raft. "I'm just not much for boats."

"Can you swim?" Caden asked.

"I can…in a pinch. It's more an embarrassing phobia."

"You're afraid of the water?" he asked.

"Why do you think I opted to enjoy the canyon by walking down the sides, rather than going through it on the river?" She forced a grin. "But I'll be fine."

"Sounds like you better get the extra life jacket," Bruce said. "Sorry, we only have one."

"Then one will have to do," Caden said, handing it to her.

She frowned. Heading downstream in these rapids without a life jacket wasn't a smart move.

"I'll be fine," Caden said, as if reading her mind.

She nodded her thanks, then tugged on the bright orange jacket. She just wanted to get this over with. All of this.

Caden caught her gaze. "All we need to do is get through a couple miles of rapids ahead, and we can call the authorities."

Unless they capsized in the rapids.

Or the men after them had an ambush set up.

Or both.

She tried to push away the negative thoughts. Normally, she was someone who always saw the glass as half-full, never half-empty, but this situation was trying pull her into a dark place she had no desire to go.

I need courage right now, God.

The men quickly moved their equipment, giving Caden and her room on the inflatable seat.

"Up ahead is going to get pretty rough," Bruce shouted above the loud roar of the water. "We need to make sure the boat doesn't flip. Which means if we get high-sided, I'll say the word, and we're going to need to throw our weight toward the downstream tube of the raft."

Gwen clutched onto the handles on the side and made sure her feet were secured in the foot braces as the men quickly went through more instructions. How to hold the paddle properly, what to do if she got thrown out and, most of all, a reminder not to panic.

Right. Don't panic. Except she was already there.

It took all her concentration to paddle as they worked together to keep the raft upright. She drew in a deep breath. The steep rock walls of the canyon rose up on either side of them as they started down the narrow river. The churning water surged past large boulders that were scattered down the narrow waterway. She'd read the warnings about this area for its Class III rapids, and this was why. She drew in another deep breath. Ahead of them, white foam churned where there were sudden drops in the water level and narrow stretches that required navigating between the large rocks.

"You okay?" Caden asked.

She nodded, but she really wasn't. The river had them bobbing downstream in the current, leaving her feeling totally out of control. And the rapids swirling around her terrified her almost as much as the men after them, if not more.

"You've got to be in pretty good physical shape to hike these canyons." Caden maneuvered his paddle beside her.

"And you're wondering why someone who's athletic is afraid of the water?" she asked.

"It did cross my mind."

Water sprayed across her face as the river began to narrow and the white foam of the rapids increased. She braced herself for impact as the raft bumped into the side of a large boulder, shifting their trajectory downstream. She worked to stay in sync with the three men as they shoved their oars into the water to compensate, while her memories rushed through her.

She'd almost drowned that day. All it had taken was a few feet too far into the sea for it to start pulling her out instead of pushing her back onto the shore.

"Gwen…" Caden's voice yanked her to the present. "Hang on."

She grasped onto the ropes on the side of the raft and ensured her feet were secure. The back of the raft where they were sitting rose out of the water. She felt her body slide forward, but managed to hang on. She was going to be fine. They all were. They would get within cell-phone range, call for help and this would be over. Whoever was after her wasn't going to win. Just like the canyon wasn't going to win. Not today.

The raft pitched again, this time throwing her into the air. She lost hold of the raft's safety rope that wrapped around the exterior and tried to grab onto it again, but missed. A second later she felt her body hit the water. She was falling as the current pulled her down the river. Her body slammed into one of the rocks, scraping her back against something as she fought to stay above the waterline. Fought to breathe. But she was moving too fast. She could see the raft bobbing in the swirling white water just beyond her, but she couldn't reach it.

Her mind went over the instructions Bruce had given them. Don't try to swim or stand up. She turned onto her back, feet first, like he'd said, and tried not to panic as she felt herself being pulled under.

Caden watched as the raft buckled and Gwen slid into the water. A rush of panic swept through him. They wouldn't be able to slow down for another hundred feet, where the water calmed down again. Swimming after her might be their last option, but they had to try something.

He yelled at the other men. "Do you have a throw bag? We've got to get her out of there."

"Under your seat. We'll try to get you as close as we can."

He pulled out the standard rescue equipment, including a coil of rope that could be thrown into the water in a rescue scenario, while the other two men worked to steer the raft toward her while keeping it from totally flipping.

While he might not have good memories of Gwen from his past, he certainly didn't want anything bad to happen to her. And besides, it was obvious from the time they'd spent together that they were both different people from when they'd known each other all those years ago. Both of them had grown up.

All of a sudden she was gone.

He shouted at the other men. "Do you see her?"

He scanned the water in front of them, then the shoreline, as the panic began to seep in. He was surprised at the urge to protect her that rushed through him. She had a life jacket on, but even that couldn't guarantee she wouldn't be pulled under. And if she was already afraid of water and panicked...

He shoved down the fear, focused instead on simply finding her.

Where was she?

Seconds passed. The raft went down another drop into a pool of calmer water.

"There she is," Bruce shouted. "On those rocks on the shoreline."

Relief flooded through him as he caught sight of her. Somehow, she'd managed to pull herself to the edge of the water. They fought against the current to steer the raft toward the shore.

"Gwen!"

He jumped out and hurried across the rocks to where she was lying on the shoreline, half of her body still in the water.

"Gwen—Gwen, are you okay?"

He pulled her up out of the water. She sat next to him, breathing hard from the exertion.

"I just... I need to catch my breath."

"Are you hurt?"

"I don't think so, though I scraped my leg on something."

He checked her out quickly and found a second large scratch running up her calf, but what worried him the most was that she was shaking from the cold. He needed to get her warm.

Bruce and Levi secured the raft, then jumped onto the shoreline next to them.

"We've got a thermos of hot coffee," Bruce said, "and a thermal blanket."

Caden took the blanket, then turned to Gwen. "I want you to take off your shirt and put on my fleece. I'll hold up the blanket while you change. You're soaking wet and you need to get dry and warm."

She nodded, still shivering.

"Thank you," she said as soon as she'd changed.

He wrapped the blanket around her shoulders, then poured a cup from the thermos and held it out for her. "Drink it slow, but drink as much as you can."

She nodded, but he could see both the alarm and fatigue in her eyes. And how could he blame her? The past twenty-four hours she'd fallen off the side of the canyon, been shot at and now this. Nothing completely prepared you for something like this.

"I can't stop shaking," she said.

"You're cold, but you're okay." He rubbed his hands against her shoulders. "Give me a second. I'll be right back."

Caden stepped a dozen feet away to where Bruce was standing.

"Levi headed upstream to see if it looked like we were being followed," Bruce said. "How is she?"

"She'll be fine, but I'd like to know what you think. You know this area as well as I do. What if we stayed here, and the two of you went ahead and called for help once you were in cell-phone range? I know she's afraid, but I'm worried about her physically, as well."

Bruce glanced out at the water rushing by in front of them. "If that's what you want, we'll do that for you, but we're only a couple miles from phone signal. If you continue with us, you'll get there a lot quicker than if you were to have someone come back here for you."

"True…"

"And on top of that," Bruce continued, "if there are men after you, and they're armed…"

"I might be in for a different kind of battle."

Caden let out a sharp sigh. The man was right. He knew that. Staying here would only give the men after Gwen a greater chance of catching up with them, and that was a risk he didn't want to take. He needed to get her out of here as soon as possible.

"Give her a few more minutes to warm up, and then we'll do everything we can to get her out of here safely."

Caden nodded. "Thank you. I appreciate it."

"Don't worry about it."

Caden went back and sat down next to her, thankful she was listening to his instructions and drinking the coffee. Right now his priority was to get her somewhere safe and warm. Then they'd be able to get the help they needed to find her brother.

"The quickest way out of here is to get back into the water and continue downstream," he said.

"I know I have to get back into that raft. I'll be fine."

He was surprised at her willingness to continue down the river after what had just happened, but on the other hand, he knew she wasn't one to simply give up.

"I'm sorry you've had to go through all of this, but a couple more miles downriver and we'll be able to get a call through. It's almost over. I promise."

She looked up at him, eyes wide and trusting. He didn't miss the irony. He was the last person she would have trusted before the past twenty-four hours, but he'd do anything he could to ensure her safety. Gwen Ryland had somehow managed to slip back into his life and turn all of his plans completely upside down.

She handed him the cup and thermos.

"Can you drink some more?" he asked.

"I think I'm ready to go."

Her cheeks were still pink, but at least she wasn't shaking as much as she had been.

Levi was making his way back down the rocks to where they sat. "I walked upstream a couple hundred feet, where you can see quite a way upriver."

"Did you see anyone?" Caden asked.

Levi shook his head. "Whoever they were, there's no sign that they're following you downriver. It's still going to be rough ahead, but we'll do everything we can to keep the raft in the river."

"Thank you," she said. "For everything."

Caden helped her to her feet, but the uneasiness wouldn't let go. Those men were out there, and he was sure they'd show up again at some point. They'd gone to all the trouble of coming after her in the night, making their intentions clear. Escaping them wasn't going to be that easy. But as a long as they kept moving, and could get the authorities involved, they'd make it.

Caden settled her into the back of the raft with the blanket still around her shoulders.

It was time to go.

FIVE

Gwen focused on breathing slowly through her nose, trying to calm her anxiety as they floated down a calm section of the river. *They* were out there. Somewhere. Waiting. Watching. She didn't know what their plan was or when they were going to strike, or even what they were planning to do with her, but she did know that the intense panic swirling through her wouldn't go away. Which meant she wasn't sure what she was more afraid of at the moment—the men after them, or the water. Either, it seemed, had the ability to win today and crush her.

She glanced at the waves slamming against the sides of the raft. On top of that, she was still so cold. The coffee and the blanket they'd given her had helped warm her insides, but it wasn't enough, and she couldn't stop shaking.

She'd read that the water temperature was about fifty degrees—far below the perfect swimming-pool temperature. She knew that water below that temperature could lead to shock, as it zapped body heat faster than cold air. And she believed it.

They let the raft coast down the river for the next few minutes in the calmer waters, just adjusting its course with the paddles to keep them away from any rocks jetting out of the water. But she could see traces of white foam ahead, where the river dropped again and started churning. It was the calm before the storm, and she wasn't sure she was ready for what was coming next.

For a moment, memories rushed through her again of that day at the ocean with her family. She could almost feel the icy sting of the water as she slipped in. The gasping for air, then the panic when she couldn't fill her lungs. It had been so cold, so terrifying. The realization that those could have been her last moments as she was sucked under. The not knowing if she was going to make it back to the surface.

"Gwen? Are you all right?"

"Sorry…" At Caden's questions, she forced her mind to come back to the present. She needed to stay focused. Needed to listen to the men, who were shouting out directions as they approached another rapid. "I'm fine."

"These river rafts are built for this kind of abuse," Caden said. "It's heavy-duty commercial grade and made for class-three rivers and up. You can't do any better out on the water."

Gwen frowned. While she appreciated his reassurance, she wasn't convinced that was going to be enough to keep them afloat in the next stretch of the river. Or enough to keep her nerves intact.

"You said you were afraid of the water," Caden said.

It was a statement more than a question. She knew he was hoping for a response, but she wasn't sure how much she wanted to tell him. And, until today, she hadn't realized how much that one incident had affected her. In the past, she'd simply avoided water. It was an easy way to not deal with memories and her fears. But today—today there was no way to escape it. She was here in the middle of everything, water churning around her like her life at the moment.

"You don't have a phobia?" she asked, putting it back on him.

"Spiders."

His answer surprised her. "You're afraid of spiders?"

"I was bit by a brown recluse when I was eight. My hand swelled up, and I was convinced it was going to be amputated. I was terrified."

"That's horrible."

"As you can see, I survived, but for an eight-year-old kid, it was a bit traumatic. And my teasing brothers didn't help."

"You know how siblings can be. Are you all close now?"

"We still have our moments, but yeah. We are."

"My brother and I are, too. Most of the time."

The raft rocked gently beneath them as they moved with the current. Another couple hundred yards and the calm of the river would be behind them. She tried to shake off the terror, but the water surrounding them reminded her too much of that day, too much of what she could have lost.

Even if this raft did get them out of here in one piece, she still had no idea where her brother was, or where the men that had seemed so intent on finding her were. Nor could she shake the fact that she'd involved Caden in all of this.

"We'd been at the ocean," she said finally. "With my parents and brother." The raft made a slight dip, spraying water across her face. She kept her focus on the tree line. "We were enjoying a few more hours of sun on our last day of vacation. The swells had been bigger than normal that day, the undercurrent stronger than I'd expected, when I walked out into the wave. It pulled me out farther instead of pushing me toward the shoreline. The more I struggled to swim toward shore, the farther away I got. I thought I was going to die that day."

"How did you get to shore?"

"My brother managed to grab me and pull me in. I remember collapsing on the sand afterward. I was cold and exhausted, and realized how close I'd come to drowning. My mother was convinced I'd drowned when she ran up to me. I was so exhausted I couldn't move."

"That had to have been terrifying."

She studied the shoreline, looking for the men who'd come after them. They could still be behind them, or, knowing how slow she'd been during the night, they could be ahead of them.

"My parents were killed a couple years after that," Gwen said. "I can't tell you how many times I asked God why I lived, and they didn't. If they'd been held up in traffic that day, or driving the other car, they probably would have lived."

"Questions like that—ones posed because of survivors' guilt—are normal."

She nodded. "I definitely learned that life is fragile.

But this… I'm not sure how to deal with this, Caden. If I lose my brother, too… He's the only family I have left."

"You're not going to lose your brother."

She looked up and caught his gaze. "You can't promise me that."

She'd heard those words from well-meaning friends while her parents had been fighting for their lives in ICU. She'd learned firsthand that sometimes bad things happened no matter how hard you tried to stop them. And now, it seemed like it was happening all over again. Her brother was her one link to family, and she couldn't lose him, too.

"I know what it's like to lose someone," Caden said. "And how hard it is to move forward because you couldn't do anything to save them."

"What happened?"

"I lost my team in a helicopter crash. I was supposed to have gone out with them that day, but at the last minute I was pulled off the assignment."

"Do you ever wonder why God doesn't always intervene?"

"It's something I've thought about a lot. What you need to know is that this isn't your fault."

"It's certainly not your fault, either," she said, "and yet you're involved."

"I chose to come after you, and I'd do it all over again. Sometimes all you can do is take one thing at a time. Which means right now we only have to think about getting down this river to safety. We'll have someone pick us up and get a BOLO out on your brother and the men who came after you."

"And if they find us first?"

"Then we'll deal with them again if and when we have to."

She nodded, knowing he was right.

She let out a low laugh. "You must think I'm a drama queen."

"Hardly. I actually think you're incredibly brave."

She shook her head. "It's not as if I had a choice. Caden, I need to get out of here. I need to find my brother."

The white water started swirling around them. She stared ahead at the churning waters. Life *was* fragile. All it took was one split second, one moment, and everything could change. The truth was that no matter what they did, there was a chance she'd never see her brother again. She pushed away the thought. Ahead of them, the river narrowed, as if it was shoving all the water through a funnel into the rapids below them. She just had to hang on a little bit longer.

Movement ahead to the left caught her attention. Trees lined with poison ivy ran along the banks beside them. She couldn't make out what or who it was, but something was definitely there.

"Caden…" she said.

The men automatically pushed their oars backward, slowing down the raft, as they'd clearly seen the same thing. There was something—or someone—ahead.

Caden quickly pulled out his binoculars and zoomed in on a narrow place a few hundred yards downriver. Rocks jutted out of the water on either side, but something stood at the edges of the river.

"It could be a bear," Gwen said.

She was right. He'd seen them roaming the river-beds more than once. But for the most part, they didn't bother hikers as long as they were left alone. He brought the binoculars into focus. No, it definitely wasn't a bear. Two armed men stood on the left bank.

"Caden...what is it?" Gwen asked, panic lacing her voice.

"They're still wearing ski masks, but I'm sure it's them. We need to cut over to the other side of the bank and get to the shore now. If we don't, we'll be sitting ducks."

Which was exactly what the men had planned.

"To the right, as hard as you can," Levi shouted.

Caden pushed against the current while automati-cally making a plan. Getting to the shore before they reached the spot where the men stood wasn't going to be easy with the strong currents pushing them forward, but it was the only way they might stand a chance to take them down. He was thankful, not for the first time, that he'd opted to bring his weapon while camp-ing alone, but he wasn't sure it was going to be enough.

"I don't know if we can make it," Bruce shouted back. "The current's too strong along this section. It's pulling us too hard downriver."

Right toward the waiting ambush.

The four of them rowed harder, fighting against the current that was sweeping them into the path of the men and away from the shoreline. Caden felt the strain on his muscles. How had this happened? The men must have somehow gotten ahead of them while they'd been resting on the other side of the river during the night and planned this ambush. And they'd planned it well. Just beyond the narrow bank of the river was a drop-off, and the swirling white foam of the rapids continued on as far as he could see.

"We've got two choices," Caden shouted. "We can try and make it into the inlet ahead, giving us a chance to fight them, or fly by them down the rapids."

Both options still left them as potential sitting ducks, but if they could manage to get to shore, they might have a fighting chance. They just needed the swift currents to cooperate.

"Let's try to make it to the cove," Levi said.

They pushed harder, fighting against the swelling water to get to the small inlet, but the current wouldn't cooperate. Another seventy-five…sixty-five feet, and the men would be on top of them. Water beat against the sides of the raft, pushing them forward toward the drop-off.

There was no way they were going to make it.

One of the men fired his weapon above their heads. A second later, the other man managed to grab onto the raft's rope, then secured it around a tree stump at the edge of the river. The water continued to hammer against the raft, but they weren't going anywhere.

Caden reached for his weapon, which he hadn't been able to pull out while fighting the current, but it was too late.

"Put your hands in the air. I want to see them now!" The tallest of the two yelled against the noise of the churning rapids below them. They were jammed against the rocks—the only thing that was stopping them from going down the six-foot drop and into the swirl of water below them was the rope and two armed men.

This time he pointed the gun at Levi. "She gets out now, or I'm going to shoot you one at a time until she complies."

"Leave them out of this," Gwen said. "What do you want?"

Caden rested his hand on her leg, signaling her to be quiet. It wasn't going to take much for the situation to suddenly spiral out of control and for the man to follow through with his threat. There had to be a way to get the advantage and put an end to this.

"You heard what I said. I'll start shooting them, or you can come with us. Now."

Caden gripped her hand. Letting them take her wasn't an option.

"She's not going with you," Caden said.

"I wouldn't try calling my bluff, because I will shoot you. Toss your weapon onto the shore."

Caden hesitated, but caught the anger in the man's voice. There was a fierce determination in his eyes. Desperation, even. But what did he really want? That was what Caden needed to know if he was going to be able to negotiate out of this situation.

"Now!" the man shouted. "Toss it over here."

"Okay. I will."

Caden followed the man's instructions and tossed his gun, with the safety on, onto the shore. The taller man nodded at the shorter man—who sounded much younger—to pick up the weapon. But there was something bothering Caden. Something wasn't adding up. Why grab Gwen in front of so many witnesses? Surely they weren't planning on killing all of them. If that had been their plan, they would have already done it. Plus, killing all of them would be a huge risk, with too many things that could go wrong. No. He was missing something. What was their motivation? Their actions weren't adding up, but he couldn't put his finger on the reason.

Was this really just an act of revenge, or was there more at play? They'd left Gwen on the canyon wall, knowing that the odds of her surviving a fall were slim. But they'd taken her brother for leverage, then circled back to ensure she was taken care of. If that was true, why not just shoot her now and be done with it? Why take her? There had to be another reason.

She pulled away from him. "I have to go with them, Caden."

"Wait." He gripped her arm, then turned back to the men. "Tell me why you need her. Maybe we can work something out."

"Apparently, you're not understanding. This isn't a negotiation. You're not going to be able to talk your way out of his. Do what I say, or we will start shooting."

"I have connections," he said. "If there's something you want, money—"

"Enough!" One of the men put a bullet into Levi's leg.

The shot echoed across the water. Caden froze. He'd called his bluff, but there was no deterring the other man. And as for options… They wanted her. Alive. But why?

"Stop!" Gwen stood up. "I said I'm coming."

"Gwen, wait—"

"I have to do this."

"Listen to her," the taller man said. "And if you're smart, the rest of you won't move, because I've got enough bullets for each of you."

Blood seeped through Levi's pant leg as Gwen pulled away from Caden's grip. She stumbled slightly, caught her balance, then stepped out of the raft as Levi groaned in pain. The younger man grabbed her as Caden forced himself to sit still, heart racing and every muscle tense. He had to figure out how to rescue her. He couldn't just let them take her.

He wasn't sure how he'd become so protective of her, but she'd somehow managed to get under his skin. Gwen Ryland was the one woman, next to Cammie, that he wouldn't have minded never seeing again as long as he lived. And yet here he was, fighting for her life and willing to do everything he could to save her. The thought surprised him, but in reality this wasn't about Gwen. He'd always fight for someone in trouble. It was what he'd been trained to do. To serve and protect. But this— He had to fix this. He just wasn't sure how. Or if he was going to be able to find her in time.

She glanced at him one last time as the men cut the rope. Seconds later, the raft dropped off into the churning basin below them. Their attackers had chosen the spot well, because for the moment, there was no way to stop. And no way to go back.

SIX

Gwen glanced down at her leg as she struggled to keep up with the men. Her ankle was swollen, her head throbbed and every muscle ached from the fall—even more so today than it had yesterday. Going uphill seemed far more brutal than going downhill had, but it wasn't as if she had any choice in the matter. All she knew to do was to keep moving forward and pray Caden would find her. Because at the moment, he was her only hope.

But even that lingering hope wasn't enough. They hadn't shot her, which meant for some reason she was worth more alive than dead, though why, she wasn't sure. And even if Caden did show up, he was no longer armed, which put them at yet another disadvantage. She could try to escape, but was that even possible? She couldn't run very fast with her injured ankle and, on top of that, where was there to go beyond the unmarked trail?

"Stop trying to slow us down. He's not coming after you."

She tried to ignore the implication of what would

happen if Caden didn't come after her, because she refused to believe he wasn't doing everything he could to get to her. He'd come after her. She knew he would, and if she could slow them down, he might be able to catch up. Even if he had to backtrack upriver, he was still faster than the three of them. At least that was what she was praying for.

She glanced back down the trail. What if he didn't come? The smart thing for him to do was probably make his way down the rapids, then call the authorities. Not try to track her down. There were a number of trails they could have taken, and while she'd left him a clue, there was no guarantee he'd see it.

But whether Caden was behind her or not didn't matter at the moment. Her body ached and she felt nauseous. She needed to stop.

"I have to rest," she said, struggling for air.

"We don't have time. Keep walking."

She stopped in her tracks, ignoring his demand. At this point, she didn't care what they did. "I said I needed to rest."

"It is hot, King…" One of the men pulled off his mask.

"Fine… I guess it doesn't matter at this point if she sees our faces." The man in charge pulled off his own mask, revealing his bleached-blond hair, then pointed his gun at her. "But we don't have time for games."

"I'm not playing games. If I'm so valuable, then let me rest."

"King…"

At least the younger of the two seemed to have a heart.

"Fine." King glared at her. "You've got three minutes and not a second more."

He glanced at his partner then handed her a bottle of water. "Since when did you become such a softy?"

She sat down on a rock, ignoring the men, and pulled off her shoe and sock, both of which were still damp. Blisters had started to form on the bottom of her left foot, but it wasn't nearly as bad as her throbbing ankle. And while they'd been hiking uphill for quite a while, they still had at least another thirty minutes to get to the top.

Which made her ask the question again. If they wanted her dead—like she'd thought—why drag her up the canyon again? It didn't make sense.

She studied the two men, who'd argued most of the way up. She'd figured out their names, and now she knew what they looked like. King, with his spiked hair, was both older and taller, and clearly in charge. Sawyer, on the other hand, had a baby face and didn't seem to want anything to do with roughing her up. But it was the dynamics between the two that interested her the most. Through her job, she'd learned to read people. Sawyer seemed almost sympathetic toward her, while King was quick to throw out threats and keep his hand on his weapon. If she could find a way to play off Sawyer's sympathy, it might give her an advantage. Or, at the very least, keep her alive. But in order to do that, she needed to figure out what they intended to do with her.

"What's your plan?" she asked.

"What do you mean?" King asked.

"I'm just trying to figure out what's going on here. I

thought you wanted me dead, but instead you're dragging me up the canyon. I'd like to know what your plan is."

Sawyer took a step back. "Why would we want you dead? At the moment you're worth a whole lot more to us alive."

She tried to read between the lines, but nothing made sense. She'd assumed this entire situation was because Carter Steele wanted revenge because of her role in his conviction. How was her staying alive of any value to anyone, especially Steele? Because even if she wanted to, she couldn't do anything to change the judge's sentence. It was far too late for that. And anything he managed do to her would only get him into more trouble.

"I don't understand. I thought this was about revenge."

"What is?"

"The reason you kidnapped me. Steele threatened me in court. I thought you were his hired goons."

"I have no idea what you're talking about," Sawyer said, "but this—this is about your brother."

"My brother?" Gwen's mind scrambled to put the pieces together. "What do you mean?"

"You don't know what he did?" King asked.

"If I did I wouldn't be asking. But you had him—"

"He managed to get away," Sawyer said.

Which was why they needed her. Suddenly everything made sense. Except for one thing. She knew her brother. He would have come for her.

"What did he do?" she asked.

"He's a bounty hunter—"

"I know that."

King frowned. "He was hired by a bondsman to locate a man who had… Let's just say gotten into trouble with the law."

"What happened?"

"Your brother stole three hundred thousand dollars at the scene of the arrest. Our money."

Gwen felt a wave of nausea sweep over her as the pieces of the puzzle finally started falling into place. "And I'm your way to get it back."

King nodded.

But that wasn't possible. Aaron had always been one to take risks, but stealing three hundred thousand dollars from some crooks? He wasn't that stupid. Was he?

"My brother would never do something like that."

"Then you must not know him very well, because he did."

"Wouldn't the police confiscate any sums of money at the scene? Maybe they have it."

"Apparently he thought that we would think the police took it. Except we found out they didn't. Which left the only other person involved—your brother. And we want the money back."

At least now she knew why they wanted her alive. Three hundred thousand dollars was a lot of motivation, and they were clearly ready to do whatever it took to get it back.

King glanced at his watch. "Time's up. Let's go."

She started putting her sock and shoe back on. The bottom line was that she was on her own. She had no idea where Caden or her brother were, and once they got to the top, she was out of time.

She needed to escape.

They might need her for leverage, but once they got the money, then what? They might let her go, but even that wasn't a guarantee. Especially since he could recognize them. No, if she planned to get out of this alive, she couldn't rely on anyone to come find her. She was going to have to bide her time and find a way out on her own.

The men were still arguing as they reached the top of the canyon. Sawyer stopped and started digging though his bag for something. She took a step back, ignoring the pain from her throbbing ankle. She was less than ten feet from the tree line. All she had to do was slip into the trees and disappear. For the moment, they weren't paying attention to her. The only thing in her favor was the element of surprise, which meant it was now or never. She took another step, then started running. Every step felt like she was being stabbed as the pain shot up her ankle, but she kept running, knowing that each step was another step closer to freedom.

Seconds later, she could hear them crashing through the brush behind her. She looked for a place to hide, knowing she wasn't going to be able to run much longer. The trees on top of the canyon were thick, as was the underbrush. It was the perfect place to hide, but would it be enough?

She crouched down behind the thick trunk of a tree, then held her breath.

"We know you're here," King shouted. "You can't run far and there's nowhere to hide."

A branch crunched behind her. They'd stopped less

than twenty feet away from her, searching the trees for any movement.

"Do you really think you can outrun us?" King asked. "There's no one here to save you. No one."

"If you ask me, she's more trouble than she's worth," Sawyer said.

"Yes, but not only has she seen our faces, we still need her as leverage."

Sawyer took a step away from King. "This plan has entirely fallen apart. I agreed to going after the money, but now you've shot someone and we have a witness who can identify us. I didn't agree to murder."

"How did you think this was going to end?"

Gwen held her breath as the men continued to argue with each other. They were going to find her. Then they'd kill her.

Caden fought the current. Past the swift-flowing rapids that had almost managed to flip the raft, the river held its breath for a few hundred yards, but soon the water would drop again into another round of churning rapids. Which gave him about ten seconds to make a decision.

He glanced at the two men who had rescued them and forced back the guilt at getting them involved. But it was too late to change anything. They had to stop the bleeding in Levi's leg, and he needed proper medical attention as soon as possible. Caden glanced downriver. He also had to get off this raft and go find Gwen.

He shouted at Bruce to help him get to the shoreline, then paddled with strong, even strokes. Seconds later, they managed to guide the raft into a small alcove. The boat bobbed against the shoreline, held in place only by a jetty of land and a fallen tree.

"How much farther do you think until there's phone service?" Caden asked, moving to where Bruce was in the center of the raft.

"I'm thinking a mile. Maybe less," Bruce said.

"Levi needs to get to a hospital, but we have to stop the bleeding."

Bruce got up and rummaged through a backpack at the front of the raft. "I've got a fleece jacket we can use."

Levi gritted his teeth and groaned.

"Hang in there," Caden said as he took the jacket.

He frowned as he put steady pressure on Levi's leg. His military training had taught him the statistics. Blood loss could kill a person within five minutes, even quicker than a gunshot wound. If the bleeding didn't stop soon, he was going to have to make a tourniquet.

"You want to go back after her, don't you?" Bruce asked.

"Yes." Caden nodded. "But I'm not sure if it's the wisest move."

"I'd want to do the same if I were you."

"What about the two of you? I'd be leaving you to make it by yourselves."

Bruce glanced downstream. "That's the last set of rapids coming up. I think I can manage getting through them on my own. After that, I can call for help."

"I packed a basic first-aid kit in my go bag," Caden said. "There should be some gauze and tape."

Levi grabbed the bag, then quickly dug around for

the supplies. "I've got some bandages, but this... We weren't expecting this."

Caden nodded. None of them had been. His week-long trek off the grid had turned into a nightmare. He glanced up at the canyon wall. The raft rocked beneath them as Bruce's fists tightened at his sides. But the bleeding was slowing down, and Caden knew what he had to do. Gwen was out there, and he had to find her.

"Contact the authorities and let them know what's going on," Caden said, securing the gauze and tape around the gunshot wound as best as he could. "I'm guessing they took Rim Rock Trail to the top, since it's the nearest trail to where they grabbed her, and the easiest of all of them on this side of the canyon, because it's a shorter distance to the top."

"I think you should go," Bruce said.

Levi nodded. "I agree. I'll be okay."

Caden stood up. "I'm sorry we got you involved. If I'd have known what was going to happen..."

"You couldn't have known," Levi said. "Go find her."

"Please, call and speak to deputy Griffin O'Callaghan at the Timber Falls Sheriff's Department when you can. He's my brother. Tell him that two men kidnapped a woman in the canyon, and I've gone after her. Tell him I'll get ahold of him as soon as I can."

Bruce helped Levi get down to the center of the raft, where he'd be the safest going through the last set of rapids. "Will do."

"And you be careful, as well," Caden said as he climbed out of the raft. "Not only do you have an injured man, you're going to struggle just to keep the raft upright."

"I'll manage. We've wrangled worse rapids than this. We'll make it."

Caden helped push the raft back into the water, then started upstream. He figured he was at least fifteen, maybe twenty minutes behind them, but on his own he was going to move a lot faster than the three of them with an injured hiker.

All he had to do was catch up, then figure out how to take down two armed men.

Caden started up the steep trail toward the top of the canyon, certain Gwen and the men had to have come this way. There were distinct signs of recent activity along the unmarked path, where a number of hikers had made the ascent. It could be another group, or several individuals for that matter, but because of the low traffic these unmaintained trails normally received, he was convinced it was them.

He kept climbing another couple hundred feet, then stopped again and picked up a discarded piece of trash. It was the same blue plastic packaging for the chickpeas that Gwen had been carrying. She must have had some in her pocket.

No. This was no coincidence. He'd teased her about eating chickpeas on the trail, and now she'd left it as a bread crumb for him to find in case he'd come after her.

Smart woman.

He pushed aside the thought, and instead studied the area closer, certain they'd stopped here for a few minutes to rest. What he didn't know was how far he was behind them. He looked up at the steep trail toward the rim of the canyon. He knew he had to be moving faster than the party of three, but he'd lost time going down the rapids and then having to backtrack to the trail's access point. If he didn't catch up with them before they reached the top, where they could drive away, his chances of finding them were going to diminish greatly.

He tried to shove away the intense feeling of over-protection he felt toward Gwen as he forced himself to quicken his pace. While he hadn't thought about the woman for years, today he couldn't stop thinking about her. Or worrying about her for that matter.

But here he was, pushing his limits physically as he hurried up the steep mountain trail and praying he could find her in time.

His heart was pounding by the time he got to the top of the trail an hour and a half later. He checked his cell phone, even holding it up above his head, but there was still no reception. The trail at this point forked, with one branch following along the top of the canyon, and the other one heading west and eventually running into a road. Logic told him they'd headed for the road. He quickly drank from his water bottle, then reached into the side of his backpack for an energy bar. The effects of dehydration—muscle cramps, dizziness and nausea—weren't something to play with, and he couldn't afford to get sick, especially considering how the lack of sleep the night before had added to his fatigue. He studied the ground in front him at the junction. Something had happened here. One had veered off to the left while two had gone straight.

What had happened?

Had one of the captors left, or had Gwen managed to escape? He studied the footprints again. The single set of prints indicated a limp. Definitely Gwen. She'd attempted an escape. He hurried down the trail, then stopped when the three sets of footprints converged again. He squatted in the middle of the trail and studied the footprints again. Had they found her? He still wasn't sure.

While his body wanted to rest after the long, rapid hike up the canyon, he pushed himself forward, ignoring the burning in his calves and the pressure against his chest as he followed the footprints.

Noise ahead of him caught his attention.

She was running just inside the tree line. But she wasn't alone. One of the men who had grabbed her was running after her.

He had to get to her first.

SEVEN

Gwen stifled a scream as Caden pulled her behind the trunk of a thick tree. She faced him, adrenaline pumping through her, along with relief that he'd found her. He lifted a finger to his mouth, signaling for her to be quiet as he pulled her down to the ground.

"Stay down. Don't move."

She nodded, but she wanted to keep running, to scream—anything to stop the nightmare she'd been thrust into. This had become a game of cat and mouse, and she had no idea how to escape.

Instead, with her heart pounding, she followed his directions. She'd hoped Caden would come for her, but never thought he really would. And why should he? He didn't owe her anything. It would have been just as easy for him to continue downriver on the raft and simply call the authorities and let them deal with everything that had happened. Instead, he'd not only backtracked up the canyon and found her, but he'd also more than likely just saved her life.

At least, that was what she was praying.

An eerie quiet surrounded them, except for the footsteps of the men stumbling through the thick brush twenty yards to their left. Still stalking. Still searching.

"We know you're out there. There's nowhere for you to go. Nowhere for you to run."

Caden took her hand and squeezed her fingers, willing her, she knew, not to move. But she was certain they could hear her heart pounding as it pulsed in her ears. He was right. She'd tried running again once. At least if they stayed still there was no way for the men to see movement.

"Come on, Gwen. We're getting tired of the game. Come out before I lose my patience."

The muscles in her legs were cramping, but she still didn't move. The only thing keeping her alive was the fact that they needed her. Without Aaron, she was their only access to the money. But how long could this go on? They'd shot Levi, and now Caden's life was in danger, too. If someone died… No. They had to find a way to put an end to this.

With no other options, they waited in silence as the seconds ticked by and the men continued searching farther away from them in the dense trees.

"I think they're gone." Caden turned to her and brushed something off her face. "Are you okay?"

She shook her head. "They won't stop looking for me. Not until they find me."

"I need you to take a deep breath. I found you, Gwen. And you're okay. Just take it slow. In…out."

She felt ridiculous for falling apart on him. But she'd never had to run for her life. Never had someone take her at gunpoint and threaten to kill her. She drew in another breath and let it out slowly, trying to push back the panic mushrooming out of control.

"I'm usually more…composed than this," she said.

"Like all the other times you've had a couple of thugs after you."

She couldn't help but smile. "So I've never had anyone shove me off a canyon wall, shoot at me or chase me through the woods before. Not until these guys."

And she didn't want it to happen again. Ever.

He rested both of his hands on her shoulders for a few seconds, forcing her to look up at him. She caught his gaze and realized she'd never noticed the blue-gray color of his eyes, or how they seemed to change color in the light. Or how they made something stir inside her. She took a step back. She was alive because of Caden O'Callaghan, but that didn't mean she owed him anything.

Especially her heart.

She took another step. The unwelcome thoughts were ridiculous. Every time she'd seen Cammie over the past decade, she'd been reminded of the man who'd broken her best friend's heart. She'd listened to stories of how he'd betrayed her. She'd imagined him turning out to be a self-absorbed jerk. But instead, there was no hint of the man she'd created in her mind. He was the one keeping her alive. And he'd risked his life to do it.

"Did they say where they were taking you?" he asked.

"No, but they're after the money."

"What money?"

She blew out a sharp breath. "Three hundred thousand dollars."

"What?"

Her chest was heaving, her hands were shaking and she was having trouble thinking. She forced a slow breath. She had to take control of her emotions and calm down. It was the only way she was going to be able to function and get out of here.

She stared through the trees, thankful that the men were finally out of sight. "This isn't about me or one of my cases."

"Then what is it about?"

"My brother."

She waited for his reaction—clearly, he would be as surprised as she'd been. "What are you talking about?"

He listened while she told him that they hadn't been randomly targeted on the trail. That her brother had supposedly stolen money from a drug dealer during one of his arrests, and that was why the men had come after them. And it hadn't been a small sum of money, either.

"Three hundred thousand dollars?" Caden lowered his voice. "Are you kidding me?"

"I wish I were. They had him, but he managed to escape."

"And they needed leverage to get to him," he said, "so they came after you."

"Exactly." She drew in another breath, determined to get her mind focused. "What next?"

He glanced at his phone. "We need to get phone coverage so we can call for help. It looks like they're continuing to head east, but there is another dirt road to the north where we should be able to make a call and get ahold of the authorities."

"How far?"

"We should get connection on the other side of that ridge ahead, where the terrain opens up a bit. But we'll still need to stay out of sight."

She nodded.

"Can you walk that far?"

She glanced down at her ankle. It was still swollen and sore, but she'd make it. She had to.

Something rustled behind them in the bushes. Gwen's pulse quickened. She'd always been a vigilant hiker, watching out for animals and ensuring she kept her distance. She carried bear spray in case of an encounter with a black bear or a mountain lion, even though those encounters were unlikely. This, though, was different. Every noise, every rustling in the trees, was a potential threat because there was someone out there who wanted to find her. Someone who was likely planning to kill her as soon as they got what they wanted, because she'd seen their faces and knew too much.

"Did you learn anything about the men?" Caden asked.

She forced herself to keep moving. "King's about six inches taller and definitely the one in charge. He seems far more reckless than the other one, Sawyer."

"He's young."

"And he's more sympathetic. Like he's not sure he really wants to be involved in this. King, on the other hand…" She paused. "I don't think he'll hesitate to actually pull the trigger."

"He's done it once."

Gwen nodded. "Sawyer seems to have limits to

what he's willing to do to get the money. He was angry both at the fact King had shot a man, and at King's recklessness."

"All of that helps."

"Good, but I, for one, have no desire to run into them again." She checked her cell again, thankful that the terrain was comparatively level at the top of the canyon, but there was still no signal. "How much farther?"

"I'm hoping half a mile at the most."

She stopped for a moment and pressed her hands against her thighs, trying to catch her breath.

"You need to eat and drink something," Caden said, pulling his water out of his backpack.

"No. We need to keep going."

Every step forward was a step farther from the men after them.

"Drink some water, Gwen."

She nodded finally, knowing he was right. She just felt so tired. But they were almost there…

I need You to protect us, God. Please. Get us out of here alive.

And Aaron… She gave Caden back the water, then took the protein bar he handed her and ripped off the wrapper. Her brother had always been the first one to take on a challenge and never turned down a dare. His job as a bounty hunter had ended up being a perfect fit. He had just the right balance of recklessness and common sense to keep him out of trouble for that profession.

Or at least that was what she'd thought. This time

he'd crossed the line. And she wasn't sure he was going to make it out alive.

"I wish I knew why he did what he did," she said, shoving the wrapper inside her pocket. "Stolen cash—did he really think he wouldn't get caught?"

"Most people either don't think it through or, yeah, they don't believe they'll get caught. Selfishness blinds logic. He probably acted on impulse, spur of the moment, and then it was done and there was no turning back."

"Never thinking about what that effect might be on other people."

Like me.

Like Caden.

She tried to stuff down her anger, but it simmered in the background. There was no way to erase the damage his decision had caused. Instead, she finished the protein bar and stood up again.

"You've changed," she said as they started walking again.

"Meaning?"

"I'm pretty sure the old Caden wouldn't have come after me."

"I would have. You just didn't know me. Not like you think you did."

She glanced up at him, puzzled by his response. But maybe she hadn't really known him back then. Or maybe he'd just changed that much. She worked to keep up with him, determined to ignore the pain. But in the end, it really didn't matter. Their conversation had suddenly turned into something far too personal, and that was a place she didn't want to go.

* * *

Caden stayed beside her—he was worried about her ankle, while at the same time irritated at her belief that the *old* Caden wouldn't have come after her. He'd meant what he said. She didn't know him. Then or now. But the past really didn't matter at this moment. There was too much at stake to let the past come between them.

He studied her face, thankful there was a bit more color in her cheeks, but that was mostly from the sun. She needed medical care. Needed to get off her foot. But unless they wanted to risk running into the men again, they needed to try and get as far away as possible.

"I don't think we should walk along the road," he said. "We'll be too much like sitting ducks. But on the other hand, if we can get either a signal or a ride out of here, we'll be able to finally get the authorities involved."

He pulled out his phone.

"Anything?" she asked.

"I think I've got a bar." He punched in 911 and prayed that the call would go through.

Something clicked.

"Hello?"

He held up his phone and kept walking.

The call went dead.

"The signal just still isn't strong enough," he said, trying to mask the disappointment in his voice. "We need to keep going."

He bit back the sting of irritation as they continued walking along the edge of the road in silence, staying close enough for them to see any cars that might go by, and yet far enough to stay at least partially hidden. Because the longer they were out here, the longer they were going to be vulnerable.

"I'm sorry," she said.

"For what?"

"For projecting my anger toward my brother onto you. Of course you've changed. We've both changed."

He frowned. He'd been happy keeping Cammie in the past, where she belonged. "Forget it."

"You were right."

Irritation resurfaced, but he wasn't going to let Gwen pull him back to that place. The hum of a motor sounded in the distance, catching his attention. He grabbed her hand and pulled her behind him.

"Should we flag them down?" she asked.

He pulled out his binoculars, moving until he could get a clear view of the driver coming toward them. "It's a guy. In the car alone."

Gwen's fingers gripped his arm. "You're sure he's alone?"

"There's no sign of the men who took you. I think we need to risk it. You can't keep walking, and we've got to get some help."

Decision made, Caden moved out into the road and flagged down the car.

The midsized sedan came to a stop and the driver rolled down his window. "Can I help you?"

"It's a long story, but we ran into a bit of trouble and could really use a lift out of here. At least to where there are signals for our phones so we can call the police."

The man studied the two of them for another long moment. "Of course. Hop in the back. I'm headed back to my cabin, but there's a campsite a couple miles up the road. You should be able to get cell reception there."

"Thanks. We appreciate it."

He didn't blame the man for hesitating. Considering everything that had happened over the past two days, he knew they probably looked more like escaped convicts than day hikers. He opened the door and held it for Gwen to climb in, then slid in next to her.

"Thank you so much," Gwen said. "We appreciate the help."

"No problem."

"Are you from around here?" Caden asked.

"Just up for a couple days. I get tired of the city and enjoy a day or two out hiking."

"It's stunning out here."

An awkward pause followed. He'd never been good at small talk, or really interested in it for that matter. But there was something about the man that concerned him. Whatever was going on, the mountains didn't seem to have relaxed him. Plus, it seemed strange that the man wasn't curious about what kind of trouble they'd encountered.

"Are you hiking alone?" Caden asked.

"Yeah."

"I do a lot of solo hikes around here," Caden said. "At least once a year."

He studied the man's fingers gripping the steering wheel. The subtle scent of perfume lingered in the vehicle. Someone else had been in this car with him. Something was wrong.

"Like I said, we ran into some trouble this time," Caden said, deciding to feel him out. "Had a couple guys come after us with guns…"

"I'm sorry."

Caden's frown deepened. Why didn't he seem more surprised? It was as if—as if he already knew. Like he'd run into some trouble himself.

"The men are still out there." Gwen gave him a funny look, but Caden continued, "That's why we're trying to get cell reception. We need to get ahold of the authorities."

The man still didn't say anything.

Caden decided to press on with his theory. "You saw them, didn't you?"

"I don't know what you're talking about."

"Two men. Both armed. Probably wearing masks."

"I've been out hiking and—"

"They took someone, didn't they?" Caden leaned forward. "Your girlfriend…your wife."

The man slammed on the brakes. "Stop. Please. They're going to kill her."

"Tell me what happened. We don't have a lot of time, but I might be able to help."

"Help? How can you help? They took my wife at gunpoint. Told me to find a woman matching your description," he said, nodding at Gwen. "I was supposed to bring her back to them, or they'd kill my wife. I'm sorry… I didn't… I don't know what to do."

Gwen's fingers squeezed Caden's hand.

"What's your name?" Caden asked.

The man hesitated. "Neil."

"Neil, do you have a phone?"

"No. They took my phone. Told me if I spoke with anyone they'd kill her. What am I supposed to do?"

"Exactly what they told you to," Gwen said. "Drop me off, and I'll make the exchange."

"Why would you do that?" Neil asked.

"Because I don't want anyone else getting hurt."

"I don't, either," Caden said, "but there has to be a way to keep both of you safe."

Caden stared out the window, running through every scenario he could think of. The men had pushed the line when they shot Levi. How hard would it be to cross the line to murder?

"Where are you supposed to meet them?" Caden asked.

"There's a turn off to a parking lot a hundred feet ahead of us."

"I going to try and circle around. Take them by surprise. And I need you to do something, as well," he said to Neil. "As soon as you can, call the authorities and tell them what happened. Try to send help."

"I will. I promise—"

"Caden…"

He heard the concern in Gwen's voice as he stepped out of the car, but it was too late. The two masked men he'd encountered in the canyon were approaching their vehicle, weapons pointed at them.

"Get out of the car now," King shouted.

The three of them exited the car, hands up.

"Now this is interesting. Lover boy here tried to rescue her, but it looks as if your plan didn't work."

Neil took a step forward. "I did what you said. You promised you'd let my wife go."

"You didn't do what I said. You clearly told him about your wife. I should just shoot both of you."

"Let them go," Sawyer said. "They can't identify us, and we can bring the boyfriend with us to ensure she behaves."

"Get his wife, then tie them both up—"

"You said you'd let us go," Neil said.

King stepped in front of him. "You'll be found. Eventually. But by then we'll be long gone. So forget trying to do anything heroic, or it will be the end of the line for both of you."

Sawyer returned a moment later with the woman and a fistful of twine and zip ties. She'd been crying. Mascara ran down her cheeks as she stumbled toward her husband.

"Tie them to one of the trees," King ordered. "Then we need to get out of here."

Sawyer hesitated. "I don't like this—"

"Stop worrying. This will be over soon, and then we'll be long gone before anyone can find us."

But despite the confidence in his voice, it was clear that they were working without a plan. And that things were spiraling out of control. The situation was going to come to a tipping point and there was no way to know how they would react. Or what was going to happen if Caden and Gwen pushed them too far.

EIGHT

Gwen tried to pull away from King's grip, but he simply squeezed her tighter. Pain shot up her arm. The entire situation felt oddly surreal. Part of her still hoped she'd somehow wake up and the past forty-eight hours would end up being nothing more than a bad dream. But there was also a feeling of determination fighting to surface, because she knew this was all too real. She drew in a ragged breath. She wasn't going to let these men win.

She couldn't.

She glanced at Caden as they were marched toward the van, praying that someone, somehow, would show up and intervene before they got inside. She'd been certain if Caden hadn't found her, they still would have tracked her down. But now—now it was starting all over again.

And it was the unknown that terrified her.

"Where are we going?" she asked.

"Just shut up and keep walking."

King bound her hands behind her with a zip tie, then shoved her into the back of the van. A moment later everything went dark as he pulled something over her eyes, then quickly secured her to something inside the van.

"Stay still, and if you give us any trouble, your friend here dies."

She knew he was serious about the warning. The only comfort in the situation was that she could feel the warmth of Caden's body next to her, as if he was still trying to protect her. And now his heroics might very well cost him his life.

She struggled to breathe in the darkness, and for a moment she felt as if she was drowning. Enclosed in darkness, like she had been in the river. Feeling the water pressing in around her with no idea which way was up or how to escape the nightmare.

She forced herself to take in slow, deep breaths and started praying. Her faith hadn't always been as strong as it was now. The death of her parents had felt like a stab to her soul, as she'd been forced to navigate a situation she'd had no idea how to deal with. At the beginning, most days had felt like she'd stumbled into an alternate reality, where everything she'd known and loved was gone. And she'd blamed God for not stepping in. Getting back on her feet hadn't been easy. It had been like walking blindfolded on the edge of a cliff, praying every day she didn't fall off. And while the pain wouldn't ever vanish completely from the loss, she'd clung to her faith and as the years passed, she'd begun to feel a strength she'd never thought possible.

But what happened when it suddenly felt as if her world was falling apart again? Why was it so easy to blame God for other people's actions? To hold Him responsible for not healing a loved one or stopping some-one's brutal actions? Faith should never be based on circumstances, but that didn't always make the journey easy, or stop one's faith from faltering at times. She'd heard more than once how God was never taken by surprise, but she hadn't been prepared for this.

I don't know how to do this, God, but we need a way out of here.

One of the men started the engine and pulled out of the parking lot before starting down the bumpy gravel road. She could feel each bump. Each jostle of the van. She had no idea where they were going or how this would end. The only good thing was that Caden was with her, but even that just instilled guilt within her. He shouldn't be here.

She pressed her shoulder against Caden, was sur-prised the men were keeping them together, but escape wasn't going to be easy at this point. Not in a mov-ing vehicle while bound and guarded by armed men.

Caden leaned closer. "Are you okay?"

His calming voice pulled her back to reality. "I think so."

Which wasn't completely true. Her heart was pounding, perspiration beaded on the back of her neck and every muscle in her body ached. But she was alive. They were both alive. Maybe that was all that mat-tered at this moment.

"I thought they were going to kill me," she said, barely above a whisper. "Why do you keep coming to save me?"

"I suppose I could have continued downriver. I've

always loved white-water rafting and never miss an opportunity to hit the rapids."

"Very funny. I'm serious."

"So am I. I know you still probably don't like me, or at the least would rather have just about anyone else as your knight in shining armor coming to your rescue—"

"You know you didn't exactly rescue me. I mean, I am tied up in the back of a van."

"Touché. But this is far from over. I promise."

"Can you get loose?"

"I'm trying, but it's going to take time."

"Which is something we don't have. What happens once they're done using me to get what they want?"

There was a long pause between them, as if he was trying to figure out how to respond. They were already at a huge disadvantage simply with her being injured, and on top of that, she had little experience with a weapon and didn't know the terrain well. If anything, she was a complete liability.

"So, do you have a brilliant plan?" she asked.

"I'm working on it. It makes sense now why they weren't trying to kill you like we thought at first. They need you alive if they want to get to your brother and the money."

"Yes…"

"Which buys us some time." Caden shifted next to her as they went over another bump in the road. "Do you know where the money is?"

"No. He never said anything about it to me. Actually, I don't really know if he has the money. Only that they're planning to make an exchange."

"Do you know when?"

"No."

Which meant Caden was expendable. And eventually she would be, as well. He was only someone to make her behave in the meantime, but when all of this was over, no matter how Sawyer felt about murder, she was certain neither of them was going to survive if they didn't find a way to escape.

And neither would her brother.

All for money.

"We need to get out of here," she said. They went over another bump and she hit her head on the side of the van.

"Agreed, but at the moment our options are limited. Levi and Bruce will get ahold of the authorities as soon as they can get a cell signal, and someone will find that couple eventually."

But *eventually* might not be soon enough.

"How was Levi when you left them?"

"We managed to get the bleeding to stop, but he's in a lot of pain. They were facing a rough ride down that river."

Hopefully, they'd already gotten to help, and the authorities were looking for her and Caden, but it could take days to find them. How many people's lives had been affected by her brother's actions?

The van slowed down. She could hear the tires crunching on the gravel. Metal hinges creaked like a gate was opening. She estimated they'd been in the car maybe twenty minutes. So they hadn't gone far. There were dozens of houses on the outskirts of the canyon. Most of them were isolated, which meant a perfect hideout. It would take law enforcement days to search the area.

A minute later, one of the men pulled her out of the van. "Let's go. Inside, both of you. Now."

"Where are we?" she asked.

"Your home away from home for the next few hours, but just remember this—the more you cooperate with us, the easier this is going to be. Try to pull something and your boyfriend here is dead."

Caden's initial reaction was to try and overpower the men as they stepped out of the vehicle, but he knew it wasn't a wise move. Not at this point. Not when he'd been unable to undo his hands, and he still couldn't see. He was going to have to bide his time and wait for an opportunity. The problem was time wasn't on his side. Once Bruce and Levi called the authorities, he knew they would start a search, but narrowing down their location was going to be tedious. Which meant the men who had captured them still had the advantage.

The men left on their blindfolds as they walked toward the house, and he tried to orient himself. A bird called out and a dog barked, but there was no sound of cars or traffic. More than likely they were still somewhere fairly remote, in one of the surrounding houses. While he always camped when he came here, there were plenty of options depending on how much you were willing to spend. Anything from million-dollar houses with heated floors and spectacular mountain views costing hundreds a night, to small cottages perfect for a romantic getaway. All of them gave you a chance to retreat to a remote part of the state.

One of the men sat him down on something solid, then pulled off the blindfold before quickly rezip-tying his hands to the arms of the chair. Caden blinked at the brightness from sunlight streaming through the windows of the house, then waited for his eyes to adjust.

He glanced at Gwen, who was sitting beside him, and caught the exhaustion in her eyes. The only positive thing about the situation—if he could even call it positive—was that she wasn't out on the trail anymore, because he wasn't sure how much longer she could have continued running. But this—this wasn't the solution he'd been looking for.

Shoving aside his frustration, he glanced around the room, needing to take in as much as possible so he could start making a plan. The dining room where they sat was part of a large open floor plan connecting to the living room and kitchen. A glance behind them showed two-story windows that led to a large wooden balcony with incredible views of the surrounding forests and mountains. Caden frowned. He wasn't sure how these guys had managed to snag this house, but he had to give them credit for finding something so isolated. And with little time to prepare, they had to have a connection to the owner. But finding them was still going to be difficult and more than likely the nearest neighbor wouldn't hear a gunshot, let alone a scream.

King stepped in front of Gwen. Caden's muscles tensed.

"I figure if anything will get your brother to respond, this will." King held up her phone. "What's the code?"

Gwen hesitated.

He turned his gun on Caden. "I said what's the code?"

"Two-two-nine-four."

"Now was that so hard? Look up at me."

King snapped a photo. "Your brother's foolishness is going to cost you your life if he doesn't follow through."

"What is your plan?" Caden asked.

"I thought that was obvious. You—*her*—for the money. You're just motivation for her to cooperate with us, so her brother will give us what's rightfully ours. As soon as we can arrange a meeting place, we'll make the exchange, and this will all be over." King's own phone rang. He picked it out of his pocket and frowned. "I'll be back."

Sawyer stood in front of them, looking uncomfortable with the situation, something that could work for them. If Sawyer was more sympathetic, they needed to find a way to play off that and somehow gain his trust. And perhaps manipulate his guilt at the same time.

"She needs something for the swelling in her ankle," Caden said as soon as King was out of earshot.

Sawyer frowned. "I'm not a doctor. What am I supposed to do?"

"Just get her some ice. There has to be something in the freezer. Please."

Sawyer hesitated, then pulled open the door of the large freezer on the other side of the open counter. He rummaged around for a few moments, then pulled out a bag of frozen peas and held it up.

"That will work fine," Caden said.

Sawyer propped her ankle on another chair, then set the bag on her ankle.

"Thank you," Gwen said.

"Anything else?" Sawyer asked.

Caden bit back the ready comment on the tip of his tongue. He could think of a number of things he could use right now, but he needed to tread cautiously.

"No, but I appreciate your help." Caden glanced toward the entryway, where King was still talking on the phone. "Listen, while your friend's out of the room, I have to say I don't know why you're here. You seem motivated by something different than him."

"You have no idea what motivates me."

"Maybe not, but I do know that the rap sheet you're going to face when caught will be pretty significant."

Sawyer's frown deepened.

"I just want to help," Caden continued. "You don't seem like the kind of person who belongs here in this situation. Do you have a family?"

Sawyer hesitated. "Two kids and child support."

His motivation.

"So you're just looking to take care of your kids," Gwen said.

"Yeah."

"I get where you are," Caden continued, "but you need to put a stop to this for their sake if nothing else. You don't want your kids to end up with a father in prison for the rest of his life. There are far better ways to earn a living. Trust me."

"I tried the honest route, and there's not a lot out there for someone like me. Minimum wage doesn't exactly pay the bills."

"You're right, it doesn't, but—"

"Stop trying to figure me out." Sawyer held up the gun, but his hand was shaking. "You don't know anything about my life or who I am. Nothing about why I'm here right now. All I ever wanted was to take care of my family, but things happen."

"You still don't have to be involved in this."

"In case you didn't notice, I already am."

Caden let silence settle between them, then chose his words carefully. "My connections could help. My brother's in law enforcement. All you'd have to do is call him. We'd tell him how you helped us, and I can guarantee they'd be sympathetic to you. Up to this point, no one has died, but if that changes—if you're looking at murder—it's going to be harder to fight something like that. And prison—that will become inevitable at that point. There's no turning back once you cross that line."

"We're not going there, and we won't get caught."

"Are you sure?" Caden leaned forward while Sawyer started pacing in front of him. "Have you really thought about what you are going to do when this is over? Try to disappear with your kids? Because the authorities will track you down. And, I'll be honest, there's something else that should bother you."

Sawyer stopped in front of him. "What's that?"

"Do you really think King's going to share that money with you?"

"What...? Of course he will."

"I don't know. He seems more like the kind of person who wouldn't think twice about betraying someone. And for all that cash... All I'm saying is that fifty percent won't go as far as the entire amount. It would be enough to disappear. All he'd need to do is make you disappear first, and this is the perfect setting." Caden gauged the other man's expression and decided to push harder. "It would be simple to dispose of a body so it wouldn't be found for years…perhaps never."

"Stop!" Sawyer stumbled backward. "You don't know what you're talking about, but I promise that I'm not going to be the one whose body will be found."

Caden backed off at the threat, not wanting to push the man too far. It was clear from his body language he was already panicking.

"What's going on?" King walked back into the room, then dropped his cell phone on the kitchen counter in front of them. "What are you doing?"

"Her ankle's swollen," Sawyer said. "They asked for ice."

"So all of a sudden you're their butler."

"No, I just thought—"

"No, *that's* the problem. You didn't think. We're not here to cater to their wants and needs. We're here for one reason, and one reason only."

"We need to talk." Sawyer pulled King aside, but not far enough out of earshot that Caden couldn't follow the conversation. "This isn't what I signed up for. There are witnesses that can identify us. If the authorities find us—"

Caden glanced at Gwen. Maybe he had gotten through to the man.

"You're welcome to walk away if you don't want to take the risk. If you don't want your half of the money—"

"Of course I want it, but it was supposed to be simple. No one was supposed to get hurt. If the authorities find us now—after kidnapping them, plus, the man you shot—we're going to prison for a long time."

King's jaw tensed. "Is that what they've been telling you? Scaring you with their theories—"

"No."

"Last time I looked we're the ones with the guns, and they're the ones tied up in chairs. Stop worrying. This will be over soon, and you'll have your cut. After that, I don't care what you do."

"But—"

King held up his hand. "Enough."

King turned to Caden and kneeled down in front of him, so he was at eye level. "You're here for one reason, and one reason only, and that is to ensure she cooperates. To be honest, at this point, my patience is almost finished. So you will do exactly what you are told to do and nothing further. Do you understand?"

Caden nodded, but the seeds of dissension had already been planted. Now he just had to pray that they would come to fruition.

"And you…" he said, turning to Gwen. "You better hope your brother calls back."

NINE

Gwen glanced at the clock on the microwave. An hour had passed since King had sent the photo to her brother, and so far, there had been no response. Which had her worried. She had no idea where her brother was, or why he hadn't responded. She had no details on what had actually happened when he'd escaped, but at least he was alive. She also knew him well enough to be sure he would have come looking for her to find out if she was alive. He had to be somewhere nearby. But the message. It was possible he was still in the canyon with no cell phone reception, but if not, why hadn't he answered the message?

Right now their own escape seemed impossible. The men had tied both of them to the solid wood chairs, and trying to get loose had only managed to rub her wrists raw. Conversation between her and Caden was limited, while King and Sawyer continued to argue. She could tell they were nervous, and as far as she was concerned, they should be.

She turned to Caden, glad that for the moment, the men didn't seem to be paying attention to them.

"Do you think you can get loose?" she asked.

"Not easily. The guy knows how to secure someone."

"I was hoping your training would have given you some…secret way to escape."

"Don't worry. I'm not giving up."

But she caught the expression on his face and knew he was worried. She felt guilty, knowing he was here because of her. No matter who he'd been before, the man had integrity and courage, not to mention he wasn't bad-looking, either.

She stopped the nervous laugh from erupting, then quickly shoved aside the ridiculous thought. Knights in shining armor came in all kind of packages, but in real life—unlike in a fairy tale—it didn't mean you were obligated to a happily-ever-after ending with them.

Especially if that knight was Caden O'Callaghan.

"Why hasn't he answered?" Sawyer's raised voice broke into her thoughts.

"Be quiet." King had his back turned toward them, but his answer was still loud enough that she could hear him. "They won't find us. No one can trace us here. They have no idea which way we went and can't lead anyone to us. Without taking risks, we will have nothing."

Sawyer clearly wasn't convinced. "Except this isn't what we agreed to. We were going to follow him and take him. No one hurt. And if the brother doesn't respond, all of this will have been for nothing."

King hesitated. "Then we'll have to get rid of them, but for now, we have everything to gain."

Get rid of them.

Their voices dropped off to where she couldn't hear them anymore, but she'd heard enough and what she'd heard chilled her.

She pulled on her hands. "Caden…"

"I heard them. We just have to wait for the right time. They'll make a mistake."

"What about a plan? I'm not sure that turning them on each other is going to be enough."

"Sawyer thinks they've already gone too far. That's to our advantage. Hopefully he'll keep King in check."

"And if he doesn't?" she asked. "Because I don't think the man is bluffing. King's definitely the one in charge. If Aaron doesn't answer soon—"

"All that matters for now is that they need you. It's the only way your brother will turn over the cash to them and they know it. We'll figure this out, Gwen. I promise. Trust me."

Trust me.

How could she trust the man who'd devastated her best friend? And yet, how could she not? He'd gone out of his way to rescue her and protect her when he could have simply waited and called the authorities. He'd risked his own life and come after her. She nodded, realizing that as crazy as it sounded in her mind, she did trust him. And at the moment, she couldn't imagine anyone else she'd rather have on her side in this situation.

"I'm assuming you've been in situations like this?" she asked.

"Tough situations, yes. Situations with my life in danger, yes. But kidnapped…no."

"What happened?"

She saw the muscles on his face flinch, and realized she'd struck a nerve. Her questions had been too personal, and yet, she needed some ray of hope that they were going to get out of here alive.

"I spent time working in military intelligence, as well as Special Forces, so there was more than one situation where I wasn't sure I'd make it out alive."

"And yet you did."

"Thankfully, yes, though I wasn't sure at the time. I decided God still needed me around for some reason."

"I'm glad."

"Me, too." He turned and caught her gaze. "I'm not going to make you any promises that this will end without anyone getting hurt. I can't do that. But I can promise that I will do everything in my power to keep you safe. Just follow my lead."

She nodded as King and Sawyer walked back into the room a moment later, both frowning. Her stomach churned as she tried to stuff down the panic. She had no doubt they would get of rid both of them, if they were no longer needed. But what would they do if her brother didn't call?

King grabbed one of the chairs, sat down across from her and leaned forward. "I'm struggling a bit, trying to imagine what's going through your brother's mind right now."

He paused, as if waiting for her to say something. But while she had the same questions, she had no desire to interact with the man.

"I'm pretty sure he wouldn't have gone to the police," he continued when she didn't respond. "That would be far too risky, because they would find out what he did, and once that happens, he'll lose everything. So knowing he's a bounty hunter, used to handling things on his own, I'm trying to figure out what he's thinking."

She pressed her lips together, still not sure where he was going with the conversation.

"I would have assumed all along," King continued, "that he would have been worried about what happened to you and come back here. He could be searching for you right now, which also means—depending on where he is—he might not have phone coverage. That would be one explanation of why he isn't responding. The other option is that I judged him wrong, and he really doesn't care what happens to you. Meaning he cares more about the money now in his possession than his sister."

He paused again, letting his horrible suggestion gain traction. Her mind started reeling with the consequences of the situation. Because like it or not, the jab struck, just like King had wanted it to. She'd been running the same scenarios through her own mind. Her brother couldn't go to the authorities for help without them finding out what he'd done, and even if he did, he had no idea where she was.

But Aaron *would* come for her, she had to believe that.

"Tell me about your brother," King said.

She hesitated, uncertain of what she was supposed to say. "What do you mean?"

"Are the two of you close?"

"Why does that matter?"

"Because I need to know if this photo I sent is going to be enough motivation for him to bring me our money."

"We're pretty close. We try to take a couple weekends off together every year to go hiking. And we spend time together when we can."

"Did he tell you about the money?"

"No."

"If you are as close as you say you are, I find that hard to believe. You spent most of the weekend with your brother, and you're telling me he never mentioned he was suddenly three hundred thousand dollars richer. I'd imagine a secret like that would be hard to keep to yourself."

Her jaw tensed. "I don't know what you want me to say, but he never talked about the money. In fact, we didn't talk much about work. It was supposed to be a relaxing weekend."

"Something that didn't happen," Caden added.

King stood up and took a step backward. "Let's try something else then. If he can't go to the police or any of his informants that help him track down people, who would he go to for help?"

"I don't know."

"A best friend? Fellow bounty hunter that might help him?"

"I really don't know."

"We'll, that's a problem. He's not responding, and I'm running out of time." King glanced at the phone again. "I want you to leave a second message. And this time you'd better convince him you're worth saving."

Caden frowned. Even though he wasn't in a position to fight back, he'd still had enough of the man's intimidation tactics. "Maybe instead of all your threats, you just need to give Aaron some more time. He's probably trying to figure out what to do, just like you are."

King stepped in front of him. "The problem is I don't have the luxury of time. I need to put an end to this. Now."

"And then what happens?" Caden asked.

"Does that matter to you?"

"Considering the fact I'm sitting here, tied to a chair and having my life threatened, what happens next does matter to me." Caden chose his words carefully, still feeling as if his best option at the moment was to turn the two men against each other.

"A hundred and fifty thousand dollars is a significant amount of money," he continued, "but I'm not sure if you could disappear completely. That is what you're planning, isn't it? Disappearing. I've heard Colombia has nice beaches, or maybe Peru, where you can live a comfortable lifestyle for far less than here in the US. But how long will the money actually last? I don't know…eight, maybe ten years. With twice that, you'd be set for at least twenty years."

Sawyer took a step back. "King isn't going to cut me out—"

"No… I was just thinking out loud," Caden said.

But it was already too late. Caden caught the renewed panic in Sawyer's eyes. Another seed had been planted.

"Enough of this nonsense. Sawyer, don't listen to them. Because here's what is going to happen." He turned to Gwen. "I'm going to contact your brother again, and this time you need to make sure you get his attention." King pulled his weapon out of the holster and pointed it at Caden's head. "Because if you don't, I will shoot him. Do you understand?"

Gwen's lip quivered as she nodded.

"Good." King unlocked the phone. "I want you to convince him that I'm serious about my threats. And that if he goes to the authorities, you're dead. The choice is his, but he's running out of time if he wants to see you alive."

King dialed the number, then held up the phone, warning her one last time to do exactly what he'd told her.

Caden's jaw tensed. He was frustrated that there wasn't anything else he could do to stop what was happening. Instead, Gwen took in a deep breath and waited for the call to go through.

No answer.

"Leave a message," King said.

"Aaron…" Gwen's voice cracked. "I don't know where you are, but I need you to know that these men are serious. They are threatening to kill me if you don't make the exchange. Do what they say. Please. And Aaron—"

"That's enough." King ended the call.

Caden stared at the phone as if that would somehow make the return call come through faster.

"I can make something to eat," Sawyer said.

King dropped the phone onto the counter. "Fine."

Sawyer started pulling out sandwich ingredients from the fridge. A clock ticked off seconds above the stove, while the TV ran muted in the background on one of the kitchen counters. Caden could only imagine what Gwen was thinking. Fear, anxiety, even guilt. It was one of those situations you never imagine happening to you. Only to someone you read about in the news cycle. And yet, this was real and if they didn't figure out a way to stop the men, it would be their shocking deaths people would see reported on the ten o'clock news.

Tensions seemed to escalate with each passing minute. Time ticking by, frame by frame, like a horror movie where you're not sure if the good guy's going to make it out alive or not. He wanted to talk to Gwen, to reassure her that they would get out of here. Somehow. He'd figure out a way. If he couldn't undo the bindings, he'd find another opportunity. It was what he was trained for—running into trouble and figuring out a solution.

The phone rang.

King snatched up the phone. "I see you got my messages."

Caden tried to read King's reaction, wishing he could hear the conversation, but King turned away from them and kept his voice just barely above a whisper.

King muted the phone. "Your brother wants to make sure you're still alive."

Proof of life.

The entire scenario seemed so surreal. How had his weekend away ended up here?

"Tell him you're fine," King said. "Nothing more."

King unmuted the phone then held it up in front of her.

"Aaron—"

"Gwen…are you okay?"

"For now. I'm here with—"

King muted the call again, then continued the rest of the conversation on the far side of the room. A minute later, he hung up.

"What did he say?" Gwen asked.

"He's a smart man. He's agreed to the exchange."

"And after you get the money?" she asked.

King stopped at the edge of the hardwood floor. "Now that is always the problem with an exchange. I don't trust your brother, and I'm pretty sure he doesn't trust me."

"So what's the plan?" Sawyer asked.

"I'll take care of the details, but we'll meet in the morning."

"And in the meantime?" Caden asked.

"The two of you will have to come with me. I need a place to ensure you don't escape again."

"Wait, King…" Sawyer's face had paled.

"What is it?"

Sawyer dropped the knife he'd been using to spread mayonnaise. "We have a problem. We just hit the news cycle."

He turned up the volume on the small flat-screen TV, where a reporter had just started talking.

"According to witnesses, a female hiker fell off one of the canyon walls yesterday afternoon, but there seems to be an unexpected twist in the case, leaving the authorities with more questions than answers in this bizarre story. Two men who make yearly trips to this part of the state claim that they encountered the woman while rafting down the river and offered to give her a ride. But instead of having to deal simply with the rapids, one of the men was shot in the leg by an

unknown assailant, and the woman was kidnapped. The injured rafter is now recovering, but the woman is still missing, and the identity of both assailants is still unknown.

"We will update the story as more information becomes available."

"They're onto us," Sawyer said.

"Don't worry," King said. "They can't identify us and they can't trace us here."

Sawyer's breathing increased. "Except your assurances aren't exactly working. You told me all we had to do was grab the guy, and we'd get the cash. How long is it going to be until they figure out who we are? Until our faces are on the news next to hers."

"Her brother would be foolish to mention us. He'd end up going to prison, and I'm pretty sure he doesn't want that. We'll be long gone by the time they identify us."

But Sawyer was clearly not convinced. Caden could see it in his eyes and the furrows on his forehead. A simple plan, they'd thought, had suddenly spiraled out of control. But whether that would work to his and Gwen's advantage or not, he wasn't sure.

"You can't guarantee that we're safe here," Sawyer said.

"Stop worrying. I said they won't find us."

"You can't promise me that. You might be able to disappear, but I have two kids to worry about. I'm not going to prison."

King grabbed a slice of cheese from the package and folded it into fourths. "You should have thought about that when you decided to do this with me, but instead you've contributed nothing and complained the entire time. And you know what else? Our hostage here was right. Three hundred thousand will guarantee that I can disappear for the rest of my life. Buy a little cantina south of the border and spend my days sunning on the beach…"

King pulled out his weapon.

Sawyer took a step backward. "What are you doing?"

King shifted the aim of his gun at his partner. "I'm saying that you're disposable. You've always been disposable. And without you—"

"King…don't—"

King fired a single shot at his partner.

Caden watched in horror as Sawyer dropped to the floor, his eyes staring up blankly at the ceiling.

TEN

Gwen's ears were still ringing as King quickly untied them from the chairs then bound their hands again in front of them with zip ties. He motioned her and Caden to move toward the stairs that led to the second floor, but she couldn't stop looking at the man lying on the floor. Her brain fought to process the situation. Anxiety pressed against her chest. She couldn't breathe. King had just killed his partner in cold blood, and that wasn't the only thing terrifying her at the moment. If King had killed his partner, she knew he wouldn't hesitate doing the same to them. Plus, they were witnesses to the murder, thus likely sealing their fate.

Which terrified her.

She pulled her gaze away from Sawyer and his blank stare while trying to push back the nausea. In her line of work, she'd seen plenty of abuse and devastating circumstances—things that she knew she would never be able to erase from her mind. But this... She'd seen this happen. And she had no doubt King would follow through with every one of his threats if pushed, as he got more desperate to control the situation.

Gwen's mind tried desperately to make sense of everything, but this would never make sense. Either the man was completely impulsive, or totally unhinged… or maybe both. Because something told her this wasn't a part of his original plan.

King took a step back, his weapon pointed at them. "If you ever doubted that I wasn't serious about going through with this, then I guess you know now."

"Where are we going?" Caden asked.

"You're both coming with me. Upstairs."

"Why?" Gwen didn't move.

King pointed his weapon at Caden's head. "I don't have to keep him around. You're the one who will motivate your brother to give the money back. The only reason I haven't shot your boyfriend here is because I still might be able to use him."

"We'll both come with you," Caden said.

"Good. Now go."

They walked ahead of him up the carpeted staircase to the second floor of the house, then down a hallway void of any photos or anything personal. Just like the rest of the house. Which made her wonder who owned this place and what it was really used for. It didn't exactly seem like the place where people spent their summer holidays, or winter vacations snuggling in front of the fire. It seemed more like a cold headquarters for a den of thieves.

King stopped in front of a large bookshelf at the end of the hallway and pulled one of the books off the shelf, then opened a door hidden behind the woodwork.

Gwen's jaw dropped.

You've got to be kidding.

"Since the two of you seem to have a knack for escaping, this is where you'll stay until the exchange in the morning."

Gwen felt a wave of claustrophobia press in on her as he shoved them inside the small room, then quickly closed the door behind them. The click of a metal lock added a sense of finality.

This was insane.

She looked around the room. At least there was a light bulb in the center, but beyond that, there was nothing more than the metal door with four walls that held some shelves with a few boxes and supplies on them.

"What is this room?" she asked, turning around.

"Looks like some sort of safe room. My father has one where he keeps his guns, to make sure none of the grandkids get ahold of them. They're also used sometimes as panic rooms, or even bomb shelters. It's pretty much just a reinforced room that can provide safety in case of home invasion."

"The panic-room description fits, because I'm certainly panicking." She stopped in front of the door. "So it's supposed to keep the bad guys out while you call for help."

"That's the idea."

"Then there has to be a way to communicate from in here, or at least a way out."

"In theory, yes." He started looking around the ten-by-ten space, then stepped in front of her and ran his still bound hands around the door frame. "Normally, like you said, they're built to keep people on the outside from getting in. There are also usually video cameras, communication equipment, and often food and water. But from the looks of this door, it seems as if he's managed to manipulate it to where we're the ones locked in."

"So there's no way out."

"I didn't say that."

She glanced around the room. Concrete walls and a steel door. No obvious escape latch. They had to be missing something.

She fought for a breath.

Caden caught her gaze. "Don't tell me you're claustrophobic."

She frowned. "I never have been before, but I've experienced quite a few new things the past couple days, so who knows."

Caden kept searching the room. "Well, you have to admit it is kind of ironic."

"Like for starters, of all the people in the world, it's you and me stuck in a safe room together?"

"Think about it." He shot her a smile. "This really isn't that bad. You could be stuck in here with King."

"Or Sawyer's dead body."

She shivered at the thought. If it wasn't such a serious situation, she'd almost be tempted to laugh. A few days ago, if you'd asked her who was the last person on the planet that she'd have wanted to be stuck on a deserted island with, she had a feeling that Caden O'Callaghan's name would have come to mind. But now…now she trusted him with her life.

She took a step back and winced as a stab of pain shot through her ankle.

"Sit down over here and let me take a look at that," Caden said.

"I don't think it's any worse. It just won't stop throbbing."

He pulled up the edge of her pant leg to reveal her ankle, then pressed on the side.

"Ouch."

"It's pretty swollen. I'm not sure if it's broken, but it's definitely sprained. And there's the possibility of a torn ligament."

"Great."

She let out a sharp sigh. He was right. The swollen area was now bruising, and the pain and stiffness had increased. While she wasn't thrilled to be locked in some room, at least she wasn't having to walk on it.

"Just sit still," he said. "Hopefully there's a first-aid kit in here."

"The ice was helping. Maybe there's a cold pack."

He grabbed two blankets and propped up her leg until it was elevated a few inches. "I'll take that along with a landline or even a cell phone, though I haven't seen either so far."

"What about some kind of monitoring system?"

"There's one by the door, but it's been deactivated."

"Do you think you can fix it?"

"I can try, but let me see about a first-aid kit first." He started searching the shelves. "There's drinking water and lots of cans of beans. Plus on the bright side, there's enough military ready-to-eat meals to last us several days if King forgets us."

"Somehow I have a feeling you ate better on the trail. I wouldn't mind eating more of that salmon pasta."

"When we're out of here and this is over," he said, searching through one of the boxes, "I'll make you dinner one night. Pan-fried, garlic-and-rosemary lamb chops—"

"Stop, I didn't think I was hungry until you mentioned garlic and lamb chops."

Caden laughed. "Well, while I can't come up with lamb chops, I just struck gold. Here's an instant cold pack."

"You're pretty good at maneuvering with your hands still tied."

"That's going to be my next project." He somehow managed to squeeze the pouch, even with his hands tied in front of him, and activated the cold pack, then set it on her ankle. "How does that feel?"

"Cold."

"Funny. And here are a couple pain relievers and a bottle of water."

"Thank you." She managed to take the medicine, but a sprained ankle was the least of her worries at this point. "Caden, if he finds my brother and the money, he won't need us anymore. Plus, we just watched him kill his partner…"

"I don't think anything has gone according to his plan. He had this idea he could grab your brother and dispose of you over the side of the canyon."

"Then my brother escaped, and I survived."

"That put both men in a predicament. But let's not go there. We're still alive, and I plan to keep us that way."

"That's what I'm hoping for, but is getting out of here even possible?"

"I'm not sure about that…yet. But on the bright side, we do have water, limited food, a dozen books and here are some games." He held up the Scrabble game. "This might help pass the time if we need a distraction."

She shot him a grin. Had he always been such an optimist? "You might not want to play with me."

"Why not?"

"I'm highly competitive at games."

"Really?"

She nodded. "Really."

"Good, because so am I."

She smiled again, surprised at how much they had in common, and at how he could make her smile even in a situation like this.

"Is the ice pack helping?"

"Definitely, and I'm fine. Really."

"You're also a terrible liar."

"Okay." She pressed her lips together. "I'm trying not to fall apart on you and turn into some blubbering baby, because honestly, I'm on the verge."

What she hated the most was the feeling of having no control and no options. She spent her life looking for alternatives in order to find the best solutions for the children she represented. Finding ways to still play inside the box while making sure things went to their advantage. But right now she felt trapped.

"On top of that, I'm nervous about what we're looking at tomorrow," she said. "I spend my days fighting within the confines of the legal system, looking for options that will better my clients, but this… I don't see any way out of this, and to be honest, it's terrifying."

"What you feel is normal," Caden said, going through another box. "There's a lot riding on all of this."

She took another sip of her water. "I just still can't

believe Aaron would do something so stupid. I thought he had more sense than that."

"Just like you're not responsible for the actions of your clients, you're also not responsible for his actions."

"No, but I am stuck with the consequences. And if King gets the money, he'll kill Aaron, too."

The room began to spin. The medicine hadn't started working, but she knew what she was feeling was from fear as much as anything. Because there was still one thing they hadn't talked about.

"He killed Sawyer, Caden. I've had to work with a lot of difficult situations in my line of work, but this… I don't know how to process this." She looked up at him. "You were in the military. You had to have seen all kinds of traumatic things."

"There were a lot of things I saw that I will never be able to unsee. Incidents that sometimes suddenly start playing over and over in my head like a video."

"How did you deal with it?"

"Not always the way I should. There are resources, but sometimes it seems easier to simply deal with it on your own. Most people see me as this tough guy who fought for his country. I've always gone into a situation, dealt with it, then gone on to solve the next problem." He sat down on the ground across from her and was now working on getting his hands free. "Ignoring what you've seen isn't healthy, and it ended up numbing me."

She studied his face, surprised at his vulnerability.

"The hardest part is when you're a fixer and believe it's always the person out there who needs to be saved and not yourself," he said.

She nodded, wondering if what he was saying came

from a place of pain. "You sound like you're speaking from experience. Is that why you left the military?"

He glanced up at her. "Partly, but that's a long story."

"I'm sorry. I shouldn't have asked."

"Forget it."

"I know you're right. Trauma affects people differently and often takes you through a wide range of emotions that sometimes come in waves of shock, fear, sadness, helplessness. I'm just going to have to find a way to deal with this once it's over."

She watched him. His focus had shifted entirely to his wrists.

"What are you doing?" she asked.

"I'm listening, I promise. I have a blade in my paracord bracelet. I'm trying to cut through the zip tie…" He held out his hands. "I just got my hands loose."

Caden pulled off the zip tie, then quickly worked to get Gwen free. But with or without the bonds, they were still far from free from the confines of this room.

"What's next?" she asked, rubbing her wrists where they'd been tied. "There has to be a way to open the door."

Gwen started to get up, but he signaled for her to stay put. "There might be a time when you're going to have to run, so you need to stay off your foot and keep it elevated as long as possible. We have to get the swelling down."

"Tell me what I can do to help."

"Honestly, at the moment, I don't know." He stepped in front of the door. "From what I can see, there's no way to communicate to anyone outside this room, and no obvious way to open this door."

"There's got to be a way to open it."

"It's a vault-style door," he said. "It doesn't seem to rely on an outside power supply that could be cut off, for instance, in a home invasion. It's also built to resist a forced entry with steel-armor plating and can be manually locked and unlocked."

He'd learned a lot about safe rooms when he'd helped his father put in one, but this system hadn't simply been made to keep someone safe. Clearly, it had been built to keep someone inside. Which in itself was disturbing. There seemed to be no wired communication to the rest of the house, and no place to view the rest of the house from the room. Breaking through the wall wasn't possible, either, as there seemed to be armor plating and a steel interior finish, which probably also meant the room was soundproof.

For the next thirty minutes, they threw ideas back and forth, but none of them worked. He pressed his palms against the metal door, frustrated, as if that move would somehow open the lock. For the moment, he was out of options.

"Why don't you take a break," she said. "We can play a game of Scrabble and forget about the locked door for a few minutes. It will distract us both."

"I don't know." He wasn't ready to quit, but still... "There has to be a way out of here. These are made to keep people out, not in."

She pulled out the game and started setting it up. "It always helps to do something different if you can't solve a puzzle."

As much as he hated to admit it, she was right. How many times had he solved an issue on the ranch while out riding in an attempt to clear his mind? He was going to need to do the same thing again today.

"First word…" She laid down four tiles. "Bore."

"Bore?" His brow rose. "That's not a description of my company, is it?"

She let out a low laugh. "Not at all. Though the setting is a bit uninspiring. I would have preferred something with a view considering where we are."

"I'll have to remember that, because if you're looking for some stunning scenery, you'd love my family's ranch. It's got some of the most beautiful views in the state."

Not that this was a first date, or that there would even be a next time. Though if he did ask her out—which he never would—he could imagine taking her on a horseback ride on the ranch, showing her the pond in the canyon, or even going for a sleigh ride in winter.

She leaned back against the wall for a moment, smiling for the first time. "Tell me about your ranch."

"Scrabble isn't enough of a distraction?" He put down three tiles.

"It's going to take a lot more than a board game for me to forget where I am right now."

"True." He noticed how she scrunched her nose when she was thinking. "There are plenty of bigger ranches in the state, but I'm proud of ours. It's been in operation since the early 1920s, when my grandparents bought the land."

"I love that," she said. "Family history and heritage. It's something I missed growing up, because I never spent a lot of time with my grandparents. And then when my parents were killed a few years ago…"

"It left you feeling alone and lost."

She looked up. "You understand."

"As I've gotten older, I've learned that I haven't always appreciated what I have. I've had friends, like you, who don't have strong family support, and I've seen how hard it can be. It's something I've learned to appreciate and want for my own family one day.

"Do any of your siblings work the ranch with you?"

"It's just my father and me and some hired hands at the moment, including a woman that uses our facilities for horse therapy classes. My brothers are busy with their own careers, though they have been known to help out when we've needed them."

When he'd been given the chance to come home and work the ranch, it had initially just been something to do between leaving the military and figuring out what he was going to do next. It had kept him busy while he worked through the adjustment back to civilian life, but one day, it hit him that he was doing exactly what he loved—spending his days working the land. And while the work was never done, and the hours were long, it gave him a sense of purpose and freedom.

He shoved aside the memories. "We've got ten thousand acres nestled beneath incredible views of Pikes Peak. Hunting, hay production, grazing and raising cattle. And what I love is that it's surrounded by thousands of areas of public land, so it's private and completely peaceful no matter where you go."

"Where is it located?"

"It's about thirty minutes outside Timber Falls."

She shifted slightly in order to reposition her leg. "I love that town. I try to stop every time I drive through and buy fudge from that little chocolate shop on Main Street."

"I know the owner. She goes to my church, and yes, her chocolate is to die for."

"I can see why you came back." Gwen laid down another word on the board. "I'd like to visit one day."

He was surprised at her confession, but didn't miss the flinch in her expression. Like she wanted to take back her words as soon as she said them. Spending more time together after this was over was hard to picture. The two of them had always been like oil and water. But then again, maybe he'd never known the real Gwen. Maybe what he'd believed—like what she'd believed about him all these years—wasn't true.

"You'd love it," he said, swapping out three of his tiles. "There's a view of the mountains on every side, and if you like horseback riding, you won't find a more perfect setting."

He rested against the wall, realizing he sounded like a travel agent. While he did love the ranch, when they eventually got out of this—which they would—he had no intention of cultivating their relationship. And he was pretty sure she felt the same. All he wanted to do right now was find a way to escape. Then he would go his way, and she, sadly, would have to deal with the fallout of her brother's crimes.

"Your family sounds wonderful," she said. "I always wanted a big family with lots of kids and cousins running around."

"Me, too."

Or at least he had. Once. Years ago, with Cammie. Now he didn't trust women—or his heart—enough to choose the right one a second time.

"And yet somehow you're still single," Gwen said.

"Reid and I are holdouts, I suppose, though I'm not sure why he hasn't been snatched up."

His brother Griffin had recently asked him about still being single. But as far as he was concerned, he was content with his life and didn't have to get married to be happy.

"You said you were doing some horse therapy. I'd like to hear more about that."

Her questions pulled him out of his thoughts, and he realized he'd missed her last move. "Wait a minute… you just scored over a hundred points."

She shot him a smile. "I always did like this game."

"And I'm realizing I need to pay more attention."

He searched for another play, wondering what it was about her that seemed to keep him constantly feeling off balance. Even…vulnerable. Something he was definitely not used to feeling. And the reason evaded him. He didn't care what she thought about him—he'd determined that a long time ago—and yet somehow that didn't seem true anymore. He owed her nothing, and yet just like he'd vowed to give his life for his country if necessary, he realized he was willing to do anything to save hers.

He switched his mind back to her interest in horse therapy. That should be a safe place to go.

"I started last year in an effort to help a single father in town and his eight-year-old boy," he said, adding an *s* tile to a word. "His physiatrist suggested therapy with a horse, but the family didn't have the money or the resources. I did a bunch of research and talked to some contacts, and in the end was able to bring the right people together. We have a woman who boards two therapy horses at the ranch and volunteers two days a week. It's ended up making an amazing difference in her clients' lives.

"Wow. I'm impressed."

"At this point, I'm not really personally involved other than offering the ranch."

Gwen studied the board and then drew new tiles. "It's interesting that you've gotten involved in that kind of therapy."

"From what I've seen so far, the results are amazing."

Gwen looked up and caught his gaze. "Have you ever thought of expanding the program?"

"At this point, I can't really call it a program. It's more of a—a test really. To see what's possible."

He studied her, wishing he didn't feel the subtle attraction between them and wondering how she'd gotten him to talk so much. Normally he was the quiet one, comfortable being with a group of people, while even more at ease alone out on the ranch.

"And yet you've already seen the results," she said. "You've got a working cattle ranch. Like with the horses, it's the perfect place to teach leadership, teamwork, life skills and accountability."

"Sounds as if you really have thought this out."

"I have."

For a moment, the game was forgotten as he focused his attention on her and wished he could ask her what was really on his mind. But maybe he was the only one feeling the unwanted tug of attraction between them.

He shifted uncomfortably on his spot on the floor. "I don't know. I've never thought beyond that one opportunity. To be honest, I don't know what all the possibilities are."

"Like I said before, I am pretty passionate about the kids I work with and tend to let my mind go a bit wild with the possibilities."

"There's nothing wrong with that. Nothing would move forward without dreams. I'm impressed with what you're doing. And I'm not just talking about the Scrabble board."

"Funny."

He matched her smile, but knew he shouldn't be flirting with her. There was simply no way to forget who she really was. He was treading far too close to the personal, a place he didn't need to go, because he shouldn't like her. Shouldn't like the way she clearly cared about other people and not only voiced her passion, but was also doing something about it.

He pushed away the memories lurking just below the surface. Maybe he'd been wrong about her, but telling her what had really happened that night with Cammie wouldn't change anything. He had no desire to go back there and dredge up the past, and trusting his heart again certainly wasn't going to happen. All that mattered right now was trying to get out of here. There had to be a way, and he just needed to figure it out.

"What are you thinking?" she asked.

"Just working on a plan to get us out of here."

"You've changed," she said, putting down another word.

"After a decade, I'd hope so."

"I meant it as a compliment. There's something about you that wasn't there before. A focus. A calmness. Besides, I never really did see you with Cammie, anyway. She's too high-strung."

"Looks like I'm not the only one who's changed," he said, realizing he was moving into risky territory. "I guess I always saw you as caught up with status and image. I've enjoyed seeing the other side of you."

"Cammie was always ready to shop, or get her nails done, or make sure she had the latest fashion. Not that I mind any of those things, but I did find that when I wasn't around her, they seemed far less important and more frivolous. I guess I was also just growing up and getting involved in a cause I feel passionate about."

"That feeling you're making a difference in your life is important. I had that when I was in the military. When I had to leave, I was lost for a long time. I was used to being a part of this larger team and mission, and when I was on my own I realized I'd lost my direction."

"What made a difference?"

"There was this old man at church. He challenged me to think about what I really wanted in life and then to not just talk about it, but write it down, and then make the necessary moves to get there. It wasn't automatic, but it worked for me."

"Can I ask you something else personal?" she asked.

He nodded, wishing she didn't both entice and terrify him at the same time.

She hesitated a moment, then said, "Do you have any regrets over not marrying Cammie?"

ELEVEN

Gwen paused again, wondering if she'd pushed too far. But what if she'd been wrong all these years about the man sitting across from her? What if he wasn't the villain in the story she'd made him out to be? She'd heard Cammie's version of what had happened that day, had sat with her friend as she'd cried for hours after the breakup. But Cammie had always tended to exaggerate *and* ensure she was the center of attention. That was part of the reason they'd ended up growing apart over the years. But Gwen's image of Caden had never changed.

Until now.

"Do I regret our not getting married?" Caden seemed to mull over the question. "At the time, I imagined spending the rest of my life with her, so it was hard, but now…honestly, I have no regrets."

She listened to him talk and realized there was another thing about their breakup that didn't make sense. For a girl with a broken heart, Cammie had recovered quickly. In less than a year, she'd become engaged again and this time had gotten married—something that had always surprised Gwen. And now, listening to Caden…he seemed over Cammie, but she couldn't help but wonder why he hadn't found anyone else after all this time.

"I know I'm prying," she continued, "but the night you and Cammie broke up… I had a lot of choice words for you. Words that while they might have been true, probably should have been left unsaid. Or at least toned down." She glanced back down at the board. "I guess that even after all these years I owe you an apology."

"Forget it. You don't owe me anything. Like you said, we've both changed. And everything that happened back then… I'm not sure it matters anymore." Caden shifted his position on the floor. "She was your best friend. You were angry, believing I broke her heart. You also believed I deserved to hear those things. I understood."

"But something tells me you don't agree with what I said."

Caden fiddled with his tiles, but she was pretty sure his heart wasn't in the game anymore. "There were a lot of things that happened that night that no one except Cammie and I know about. Things that were said between the two of us that I put behind me a long time ago."

Something about his expression told her there were still things that he was holding on to. Maybe not grief over a broken relationship, but definitely a lack of trust. Was that why he'd never married? She wasn't sure what it was, but she was missing something.

"You're not telling me everything, are you?" she asked.

Caden let out a sigh. "I haven't talked about that night for years, and to be honest, I see no reason to dredge it up now. We went our separate ways, which in the end was fine with me."

"I understand." Gwen searched for the right response. "I guess it's just that I know her side of the story, and I'd like to know yours. It's something I never gave you a chance to do before. Instead, I made too many judgments."

Caden frowned as he laid down another word on the Scrabble board. "She's your friend. It was a long time ago, and honestly, I'd rather leave it in the past."

Gwen studied his face, trying to read between the lines. "Are you saying if I really knew what happened that night, it might change how I see her?"

"I didn't say that. What I am saying, though, is that we all made mistakes and said things we shouldn't have."

She appreciated his not wanting to speak badly of Cammie, but was he trying to protect her? Or maybe he was right, and what happened was something they needed to just let go of. The situation had been extremely stressful. She remembered that night as if it had been yesterday. She'd ended up making dozens of phone calls, while trying to evade the endless questions by friends and family. People wanted explanations, and as the maid of honor, she'd managed to simply let the guests know that there would be no wedding and leave it at that. She'd never quite understand how two people she'd believed had been in love had just canceled the wedding they'd been anticipating for months. In the days that followed, she'd helped Cammie send back the gifts, dropped off the wedding dress at a bridal shop to sell and fielded dozens of questions from curious friends. It had been frustrating, but as hard as it was, eventually people forgot. Life went on.

"Can I ask one more question?" she asked.

"You can ask."

"But that doesn't mean you'll give me an answer?"

He just shot her a smile.

"Why didn't you defend yourself back then? There are always two sides to a story, but you just walked away. No one ever knew what you were thinking."

She wasn't sure why it mattered that she heard his side of what happened that night, but for some reason—as evasive as he was being—it did.

Caden rested his elbows on his thighs, the game forgotten at the moment. "I'm not perfect, and I would never claim to be. I made mistakes in our relationship, but in the end, all I know is that I'm glad that we ended things before we got married. I believe strongly—if at all possible—marriage is for life, and I'm not sure the two of us really knew what we were getting into. I would have hated for things to have fallen apart later, especially if children had been involved."

"Is she the reason you never married?" The question was out before she had a chance to think about it.

Caden just shrugged. "I've never been opposed to marriage, but I work a lot of hours on the ranch, which makes it hard to meet new people."

"I'm just surprised."

He shot her a smile. "Because I'm such a great catch?"

"Yes, actually. You're handsome, and you can be somewhat charming when you try."

This time he laughed. "Somewhat?"

She felt her insides flip. Was he flirting with her? "I do have to give you credit for saving my life twice. Though, to be honest, I'm still hoping for a third time. Still no brilliant ideas for getting us out of here?"

"No, and you ask too many questions."

"It's my job." She laughed, glad he seemed to finally be relaxing. "Plus, I've learned that you have to find time for relationships. If you're not proactive, it won't happen."

He caught her gaze. "Is that why you're still single?"

"Touché."

"I didn't mean it that way, but you did say you'd come close to getting married. Sometimes staying busy becomes a way to cope with that loss."

"I admit I stay too busy. It's easy to get through another day, then before you know it another week is gone. And then there's Seth. My ex. He lied to me about some pretty significant things. He left me with no desire to ever feel that vulnerable again. And now it…it's hard to take that first step again."

And from what she knew about Caden she was pretty sure she wasn't the only one.

"I was recently told by my brother," he said, "that I'm not one to give out relationship advice. I've tried dating some, but I always end up walking away for one reason or the other. Maybe my brother's right. I'm pretty sure that Cammie affected me more than I realize."

"Trust doesn't always come easy," she said, "especially after a relationship that's gone sour."

"True." He looked down at his tiles again. "I guess

I'm just looking for someone who loves me as much as I love her."

"She's out there."

"I'd like to think so."

"So you are a bit of a romantic at heart."

He let out a low chuckle. "Sorry, but that's not something I'll ever admit."

"I don't know. Girls like guys who are romantics."

For a moment, she wished she could take back her words. She didn't like him. At least not in that way. Clearly, the stress of the situation was playing with her mind. She'd let the ridiculous situation they were in make him into some kind of hero. She'd meant what she'd said about not ever wanting to feel vulnerable again like she had when Seth left her. When she'd found out the truth about him.

Except Caden had been her hero. He'd already saved her life more than once and she was trusting him to once again get her out of here alive. But that didn't mean it was personal for her...or for him, for that matter. They were simply two people who had been thrown together in a terrifying life-and-death situation. When this was over, she would owe him her gratitude, but nothing more.

She focused on the board that they'd forgotten about.

"I appreciate your talking to me," she said. "I know that what really happened between you and Cammie that day is none of my business."

"You're right." He put down a new word and smiled at her. "Sappy for seven points."

"Wait a minute... I thought you weren't a romantic."

"Very funny."

She grabbed her tiles and put down another word. "Seal."

Caden glanced at the door. "That's it."

"What's it?"

"Seal."

"A cute furry animal that lives in the water?"

"No." He caught her gaze. "I think I just discovered a way out of here."

Caden walked back to the wall around the door and stood in front of it. Gwen's questions had led him to a place he'd rather forget, but he couldn't think about that right now. He'd missed something. He knew enough about these structures to know that there had to be a way out from the inside, and yet while he'd searched extensively, he still hadn't found one. At least he hadn't found anything obvious. But that didn't mean it wasn't here. Because what if this safe room had never been intended to simply keep bad guys out? What if whoever owned it had another purpose in mind?

"What are you thinking?" she said.

"I've been assuming that this is just another safe room, but what if it was actually modified for another reason?"

"What do you mean?"

"Think about it. We've already talked about how a safe room typically is a place to go in the event of a burglary when your life is at stake. People also use them as a place to go during bad weather, but you always need a way to communicate with the outside."

"And that's what's missing."

He worked through his thoughts out loud. "We know that most rooms like this have a dedicated landline or, at the least, a cell phone. There should also be a radio—some way to communicate to the outside world. But for some reason, we haven't been able to find any of those things."

"Okay."

"Clearly, King could have taken any form of communication out, but that's not the only thing missing. There should also be a way out. A way to unlock the door from the inside in case someone was accidently trapped inside."

"So how did you get all of that from a Scrabble game?

"The word *seal* makes me think of something that's been concealed or hidden."

"And how does that get us out of here?"

"Something else is missing. If the purpose of a safe room is to keep you safe inside, there should always be a release handle that bypasses the locking mechanism—"

"So people don't get locked in."

"Exactly. And while I looked for one, and couldn't find one, that doesn't mean it isn't here. This room has been upgraded or modified recently. Don't get up, but can you see the paint here?"

He pointed to a section near the door.

"Yeah…it looks like it was sloppily done."

"The color doesn't quite match the rest of the room. There's also some spackling under this trim here."

"They were covering something."

"Exactly." He grabbed a Scrabble tile and started chipping away some of the paint.

"All of this makes me want to know who owns this house and what exactly they were planning to use this for," she said.

"It has to be connected somehow to the money your brother stole. Which means it wouldn't be surprising if this was used for a number of illegal activities." He turned around and walked to the other side of the small room. "There's a square indention on the carpet here, and I don't think this stain on the floor is rust."

"Blood?"

"More than likely, yes."

"And the indention?"

"They could have been storing something here. A gun locker, drugs…whatever made King three hundred thousand dollars."

"I think it's safe to assume that whatever he's involved in is illegal." She picked up one of the tiles. "But why are there games in here?"

"They could have been left behind by the previous owner. On the outside, if anyone was to look in, it appears to be nothing more than a safe room." He studied the wall where it had been repainted. "Have you ever done one of those escape-room parties?"

"No. Honestly, the thought of being locked in a room for an hour—even for entertainment—gives me the creeps."

"I did it with some friends in Denver a few months ago." He started chipping again at the paint. "We showed up at this house and were given a brief storyline of some far-fetched scenario where we had to stop evil spies from stealing classified information. The door locked behind us, and we were given sixty minutes to find the key before getting caught. It took us fifty-five minutes and, to be honest, I wasn't sure we were going to make it in time until the very end. Point is, we did. I'm determined to figure this out, as well."

"All I know is that after this experience, I don't think I'll have any desire to do that for fun."

"Agreed." He looked around the room, found a block of wood and started hammering. He knew she was nervous and, quite frankly, he didn't blame her. But he meant what he said. There had to be a way out of here, and he would find it.

"Is he going to be able to hear you pounding?" she asked.

"I assume it's bomb-blast-resistant, fire-resistant and soundproof."

Caden kept working on the wall, chipping away at the section someone had clearly covered up. "Do you know anything about the case your brother had been working on?"

"Only what I saw on the news, which wasn't much. Apparently there were several warrants issued connected to the case, and there were drugs involved, but really, that's all I know." She frowned. "I wonder if there's a way to trace them to this house."

"I was wondering the same thing. Problem is, even if Bruce and Levi go to the police, unless they can figure out the connection to King, it's not going to matter." A large chunk of drywall broke off, exposing a bunch of wires. "They've definitely covered this up. If

I can find the electromagnetic locks…" He pulled on a lever and heard the click of the lock being released.

The door clicked open.

Caden felt his pulse quicken as he stepped out of the room with Gwen right behind him. He was grateful his idea to open the door had actually worked, but they weren't out of the woods yet. While the ice pack had probably helped numb Gwen's pain, he was also certain that every step jolted her hurt ankle. At the moment, though, their only objective was to get out of here without getting caught. They'd witnessed first-hand what King was willing to do to get the money, and as far as they knew, the man was still in the house and armed. And while they might have the element of surprise, without Caden's weapon, and with her injured, they were definitely at a disadvantage.

"Are you going to be okay walking?" he asked, keeping his voice low.

She nodded, determination marking her expression. "What's the next step?"

"Best-case scenario, we escape the house without a confrontation. But in case we don't, we need to find some kind of weapon. We also have to look for a cell phone, and a vehicle to get out of here would be far better than walking. And in the meantime, I'll try to buy us some time."

"How?"

He turned back to the door they'd just exited and pushed it shut. "I'll jam the lock. Not only will he think we're still in there, but he'll struggle to open it."

He rigged it the best he could, then glanced down both sides of the hall, hesitating for a moment before he signaled for her to follow him. While he wasn't sure exactly where they were, he knew the house was more than likely a holiday retreat. And judging from the size of the place, he could narrow it down to a handful of locations. He just had to hope that was enough and they could find help.

It was quiet in the hallway as they started down the corridor. He paused, slowly opening each door. The house was fully furnished, and a pale light streamed through the windows, which meant it was already morning. He was surprised King hadn't come for Gwen yet, but there were clearly many variables at play. Had he even heard from her brother again? There was no way to know.

Caden heard a creak from downstairs and grabbed her hand. Voices sounded from below them, a muffled conversation he couldn't quite make out.

"Sounds like he's on the phone. We're going to need that weapon."

He opened another door that led to the bathroom, quickly pulled off two metal towel rods, then handed her one.

"Really?" she asked. "I was expecting something a bit more, I don't know… MacGyverish."

"MacGyverish?" He held up his metal rod. "Is that even a word?"

She shot him a grin and shrugged. "It is now."

"Do you trust me?"

"Completely."

He had a feeling she was as surprised at the confession as he was. A couple days ago, he'd still been on her Most-Disliked-and-Mistrusted list. But she did have a point. How were they supposed to go up against an armed man with two towel holders?

"If we do end up having to confront him, well... we'll deal with that. At least we're not against two of them anymore, but our priority needs to be finding a phone and some car keys."

He started down the stairs in front of her, praying the steps didn't creak.

He could hear King talking, but he still couldn't see where the man was. At the bottom of the staircase was expensive wood flooring. The room had high ceilings with thick wooden beams and a few pieces of artwork on the walls. To the left was a large stone fireplace. A glass wall to the right showed an incredible view of the mountains. On the other side of the windows, a wooden balcony extended the living space.

"He just stepped outside," she said. "He's probably having issues with reception like he was earlier."

Caden hurried into the kitchen, quickly pulled open a couple of drawers, then held up his find. "Here's a phone and some car keys."

Gwen frowned. "This was Sawyer's phone."

She was right. Making it a stark reminder of what they were up against.

"We need to get out of here—"

"Caden, wait..."

King's voice got louder.

"He's coming back inside."

Blocking their exit to the garage.

Caden grabbed her hand and pulled her back up the staircase. He'd counted five rooms on the second floor along with two bathrooms, plus access to another balcony, which as far as he could tell had no easy exit.

But while there might be dozens of places to hide, like under beds or in closets, once King discovered they were missing, he'd come after them. They needed to get out of the house. But for the moment, they were going to have to hide.

He glanced down the hallway. He'd jammed the door to the safe room, though as far as he was concerned, going back in there wasn't an option. Instead, he led her into one of the rooms and pulled her against him behind the door. He was still holding on to the towel rod, as ready as he could be. If King realized they'd escaped, or if he'd come to get them to leave, Caden had no idea what the man's reaction would be.

He tried to hear the conversation, but whoever he was on the phone with was doing all the talking. Footsteps passed on the other side of the door. Gwen pressed in against his chest. He could feel her breath on his arm as they stood as quietly as possible beside the door. He felt her heart beating against him. His arms wrapped tighter around her. The only thing he could focus on right now was the fear he wasn't going to be able to keep her safe. He fought to reel in his emotions. Everything that had happened over the past forty-eight hours had made him question so many things about his past. While he might be attracted to her, anything beyond that was ridiculous. He had no intention of falling for her.

"I think he's in the bathroom." Caden took her hand. "We need to get out of here. Now."

Still holding her hand, they hurried back down the staircase to the garage door without running into King. Caden opened the door then clicked the key fob he was holding at the two cars.

Nothing.

"Where is it?" she asked.

"I don't know, and I didn't see any other keys. We have to go by foot for the moment. Can you make it?"

She nodded, but he could see the pain in her eyes.

They stepped outside and he held up the phone.

"So no signal?" she asked.

"Nothing." Irritation wormed its way through him. "With no car and no phone, we need to find the nearest neighbor and get help."

There was no way Gwen could hike out there for long.

"Stop worrying about me," she said. "I'll be fine. I have to be."

They started walking away from the house as fast as she could go, down the dirt driveway. Barking to their right shifted his attention as a German Shepherd lunged at them, stopped only by a chain-link fence.

Gwen grabbed onto Caden. "Where did he come from?"

"I heard a dog barking yesterday when we arrived, but I didn't see him. I definitely don't want to run into him when he's not behind that fence."

"No kidding."

He didn't want to scare Gwen, but he knew there was a good chance that Fido here had just sounded the alarm. Or, at the very least, it would get King to check and make sure no one was out here.

And that no one had escaped the house.

King had made it clear that murder was definitely on the table, which meant the next time they ran into the man, they were going to have a fight on their hands.

TWELVE

Gwen followed as closely to Caden as she could, but she knew she wouldn't be able to keep up for long. Every step sent a sharp stab through her ankle that shot up to her upper leg. The swelling had only gotten worse, and before they'd left the safe room, she'd noticed that her ankle was turning a dark blue. She wasn't sure how much longer she could walk. And yet what choice did she have? It was only a matter of time before King noticed that they were gone, and once he did, he would come after them.

Her mind automatically ran through everything that had happened over the past two days as they headed down the edge of the driveway, staying among the trees as much as possible. The entire situation had left her terrified, because she knew that without Caden, she wouldn't be alive right now. She glanced up at him, surprised at how much she trusted a man she'd despised for so long. Surprised at how everything she thought she felt about the man had changed. But that didn't really change anything in the end. She still had no desire to put her heart on the line…even for Caden. It was simply too much of a risk.

She tripped over a rock and felt her ankle twist. She let out a sharp breath and bit back the pain. Tears filled her eyes.

"Gwen?"

"I'm fine."

"No, you're not." He grabbed her arm, holding on to her until she steadied herself, then bent down and looked at her ankle. "The swelling is getting worse. If you keep walking, you're going to end up doing some permanent damage."

She sucked in a lungful of air and mentally pushed away the pain. "Really. I'll be fine."

"I'll be the judge of that."

She looked back toward the house, but she couldn't see it anymore. All around them were thick trees with dozens of hiding places. King was only one person, but Caden was right. She wasn't fine. It was all she could do not to cry from the pain.

"Maybe you should go and get help," she said. "I can find a place to hide until you come back."

Caden shook his head. "And if he finds you before I get back? You'd have no way to defend yourself."

She held up the metal towel rod he'd given her. "I've still got this weapon."

"Very funny. It might have been the best I could come up with, but against a gun…"

"I'll be fine. He's just one person. He can't look everywhere. Besides, he'll assume we both left."

"Forget it." Clearly, Caden wasn't buying her idea.

"I'm not leaving you, Gwen. We're going to have to find a way out of this together."

"Caden—"

"Just a minute…" He held up the phone in his search for signal. "Finally… I've got a signal now. If I can call 911…"

He pressed on the word *emergency* in order to by-pass the pass-code protection, then called 911 and put it on speaker.

"Nine-one-one, what's your emergency?"

"This is Caden O'Callaghan, and I—"

"Caden, can you hear me…it's Griffin. I've been running the 911 calls at the station all night hoping you'd call."

"Your brother?" Gwen asked.

Caden smiled and nodded.

"Griffin." He let out a sharp huff of air. "I've never been so glad to hear a familiar voice."

"Where are you? We've got witnesses that claim you were held up at gunpoint on the river down in the canyon."

"Let's just say I managed to get myself into a bit of trouble. The problem is I'm not sure where I am right now. You're going to have to try and trace this call."

"I'll keep trying, but I'm finding it hard to track your location."

She glanced back toward the house again, distracted by the sound of the dog barking. Certain every noise was King coming after them.

"We were told you're with someone."

"I am, and she's here with me now." He glanced at her. "Her name is Gwen Ryland, and long story short,

I found her, but so did the bad guys. We've managed to escape, but like I said, we're going to need help getting out of here."

"I keep telling you, you should carry one of those GPS trackers for hikers."

Caden frowned. "My Glock has always been enough."

"Until now. But listen, I'm running a trace. Give me any details you can of where you are in the meantime."

"We drove about fifteen, maybe twenty minutes from the top of Rim Rock Trail, but we were blindfolded. We're now outside an isolated two-story house that's probably three or four thousand square feet and has a safe room on the second floor. We're a couple hundred yards from the house near a ridge overlooking the valley, and we haven't run into any neighbors yet."

"What about the person behind this?"

"His name's King and he's somehow tied to Gwen's brother, Aaron Ryland, who's a bounty hunter who stole money from him."

"Is that what this is all about?"

"Three hundred thousand dollars. Gwen's brother took the money. At least according to King, that's what happened. He killed his partner and now he's trying to use Gwen as leverage to get it back."

"And you? How are you involved in all of this?"

"I ran into her on the trail, and somehow became the leverage to ensure she behaves."

"What's King's plan?" Griffin asked.

"I know there are plans of an exchange, but I'm not sure where he wanted to meet. And we've got another problem. Gwen is injured and walking out of here isn't an option. A possible broken ankle. At the least, torn ligaments. I can't leave her."

"Stay on the line with me a few more minutes and... someone..."

"Griffin?" Caden moved toward the clearing as the call dropped. "Griffin."

"Caden..."

He heard his brother's voice one last time before the call dropped.

"Signal's gone. I lost him."

"That might not be our only problem," Gwen said, frustration seeping through her.

"What's wrong?"

She could hear the dog's barking getting closer. But what were the odds that the dog could actually track them? King would have to know how to handle the dog and she didn't see him having any patience with animals.

But if she was wrong...

"The dog. Do you think he can track us?" she asked.

"We can't dismiss it."

"What do we do?"

"In an ideal situation, we'd keep moving, but we'll never outrun him. The only advantage we have at this point is I'm guessing King isn't a great handler." He slipped the phone into his pocket. "I'll leave the phone on. Sometimes it's harder to triangulate when there isn't strong cell-tower service, but my brother will find us, and this will all be over soon. I promise."

She nodded as he wrapped his arm around her waist. One foot in front of the other. That was all she had to do. And whatever damage she ended up doing to her ankle was nothing compared to what King might do if he found them. They moved in silence through the woods, then down a narrow trail that led, she hoped, to a main road.

He pulled her closer against him and steered her over a fallen branch. She wished his closeness didn't make her feel so…so vulnerable. But it did. Both emotionally and physically. She'd always considered herself strong. She'd gone through the death of her parents, something that had devastated her and her brother. It had also forced her to become independent and make it on her own. But this… She didn't remember ever feeling so completely out of control.

With the warmth of his arm around her, she wondered what it would be like if they hadn't been running for their lives. If they were here, enjoying the stunning beauty of this part of the country, like she'd planned to do with her brother.

Wondered what it would be like if he kissed her.

The thought completely took her off guard. She had no romantic attraction to him. He'd been engaged to her best friend, *and* he'd broken her heart. At least that was what she'd always thought. That wasn't exactly the kind of man she wanted to fall for, because she knew what it was like to have a broken heart. And yet, why was it that so many things didn't add up? The Caden she saw now was nothing like the man Cammie had told her about. She'd sat with her friend for hours while she'd poured out her heart over the man who'd broken hers. There had been no signs of compassion. Nothing heroic about him.

What was she missing? Because from her standpoint, Caden O'Callaghan was a man who'd not only risked everything for his country, but had also put his life on the line for hers. And from her own checklist of qualities she wanted in a man, he was the first one she'd ever met who ticked off all the boxes.

The dog's bark echoed in the distance. It was getting closer. A new wave of panic swept over her. She needed something to distract her from both the fear and the pain, but even Caden's towering presence beside her wasn't enough at the moment to let her feel totally safe.

Memories flashed in Caden's mind as he tightened his grip around Gwen's waist, trying to help keep her weight off her foot as much as possible. She was strong. Far stronger, he imagined, than she thought she was, even though the situation had definitely taken a toll on her. He'd been impressed with her clearheadedness. So far she'd never panicked, never lost her focus, though he knew she had to be terrified. She had every reason to be.

The situation they were in had him worried, as well. The dog barking in the distance seemed to be getting louder. He frowned, determined not to borrow trouble as they kept heading away from the house, hoping to find someone who could help them. As far as they knew, King didn't even know they were gone. He let out a huff of air as he helped Gwen around a log. Griffin would find a way to track their phone and send the cavalry after them. Then all of this would be over. For the moment all he needed to focus on was getting her out of here and finding help.

He glanced at her profile, not missing the determination in her movements. But he needed to keep his focus on what was happening, because underestimating King was going to get them both killed. The man was highly motivated and had everything to gain and, at this point, nothing to lose. The only way they were going to stay alive through all of this was to escape. Because he had no doubt that in an exchange, King wouldn't play fair.

"How are you doing?" he asked, tightening his grip around her waist.

"It doesn't matter. We can't stop."

"I know this is hard, but Griffin will pinpoint our location and send someone to find us. This will all be over soon."

She nodded, but he knew she was hurting.

"What do you like to do for fun?" he asked. "When you're not working."

"Trying to distract me again?" She kept moving beside him, clearly focused on each step she was taking.

"I thought it might help."

"You're a good distraction."

He was a distraction?

"Meaning…?" he asked.

A blush creeped up her cheeks, like she'd regretted what she'd just said. "Nothing."

"I think I'd like to know what you were thinking. The fact that you see me as a distraction intrigues me."

"I just meant I've been extremely grateful I'm not out here on my own. And Scrabble wouldn't have been nearly as fun."

He helped her over a fallen log. "I also recall you referring to me as both handsome and charming."

She laughed. "You're exasperating."

"It was just an innocent question. But you've forgotten about the pain, right?"

"I had until you reminded me."

He couldn't help but chuckle. He liked how she made him laugh even in the middle of all this. Liked flirting with her even though he didn't want her to. But she wasn't the only one distracted. Having his arm around her waist and her leaning against him—this was dangerous territory. He shouldn't be thinking about the woman who'd despised him for the past decade, and yet... Why did it seem like every time he was near her, his heart raced and his palms got sweaty?

No. That wasn't going to happen. Not with her. She didn't like him, and just because he'd managed to save her life—twice—didn't change anything. Neither did the fact that he genuinely enjoyed her company despite the mess they were in. She was funny, smart... and way, way too close.

He shoved back the ridiculous romantic feelings. He was going to get her as far from here as possible—his brother would track them down via the cell phone and all of this would be over. He just had to keep her moving as fast as possible. And what he thought he might feel toward her would have to wait.

Because that was what he wanted.

Wasn't it?

Caden pushed away the indecision he wasn't used to dealing with. He needed to ignore whatever he was feeling and focus on getting them out of here. He could still hear the dog barking in the background, and it sounded as if the animal was gaining on them. They were going as fast as he felt he could push her, but he was worried it wasn't fast enough. He glanced back again, wondering if her plan of her hiding somewhere was something they should consider, but while there were a lot of places she could hide, if King had a dog, the chances of her being discovered would increase tremendously.

No. His gut told him that separating was the wrong move. Which meant they had to keep moving…and praying.

THIRTEEN

Gwen ran as fast as she could with Caden's help, but the sound of the dog's barking was getting louder. Her lungs began to burn as he steered them off the trail and farther into the thick forest, but she knew he had no idea where they were or what direction they were taking. And even if Caden's brother did manage to track them, it would be too late. King and his dog were closing in on them, and she wasn't going to be able to continue much longer—even with Caden helping her.

Caden worked to pull her closer, trying to ensure there was no weight on her foot, but her ankle felt as if it was on fire. She worked to slow down her breathing, but if King found them, there was nothing he could do. They were both witnesses to murder and there was no way he could let them get away. Even if he didn't use them to make the exchange, their death sentence was as good as signed.

She glanced behind them and caught movement in the brush a hundred feet back. He might not have located them, but he was slowly closing in, and all she could see around them was more trees and underbrush.

"He's coming this way," she said.

Caden stopped, then pulled her toward a large out-cropping of moss-covered rocks. "In here."

"He'll find us," she said.

"It's easier for him to see us if we're moving than if we're staying still."

"And the dog?"

He didn't answer as they crouched down behind the thick brush and rocks, his arm still holding her tightly. She managed to sit down on the damp ground and take pressure off her foot, while praying that the throbbing would lessen.

"This might work." Caden peered through a small break in the brush. "Looks like he's heading away from us."

"You need to go, Caden. Leave me here."

He turned back to her and caught her gaze. "I'm not leaving you."

Her heart tripped. He was far too close in the small space. It felt too…intimate. It was a feeling she hadn't expected, and like the fear she was experiencing, didn't know how to handle. All she wanted right now was for him to tell her he was feeling the same things she was. To hold her and tell her everything was going to be okay.

For a brief moment, the tension inside her eased as she explored the feeling. His strong arm still encircled her waist, while his gaze seemed to pierce through her. She knew he was formulating a plan. King might think he had the upper hand, but she knew Caden would go down fighting. He was the one thing that had kept her going. The one distraction she couldn't get out of her mind. Every time she looked at him, every time he touched her hand, or spanned her waist to help her walk, pieces of the wall around her heart had slowly begun to crumble. No matter how much she wanted to dislike him, she couldn't. Instead, she imagined what it would be like to see him again after this was all over. To visit the ranch he'd told her about and meet his family. To go on a long horseback ride with him through the mountains. He made her feel safe. Made her not want to give in to the fears no matter what was going on.

Made her want him to lean down and kiss her and never let her go.

She tried to read his expression, wondering if he was feeling the same thing she was. How, in the midst of terror, had her heart been pulled in this direction? Maybe it was nothing more than a needed distraction from the situation they were in, because she and Caden…that was never going to happen.

But if that was true, then why couldn't she shake this feeling inside her? This crazy feeling that she shouldn't just dismiss whatever was going on between them.

"Gwen, I—"

"Did you ever play hide-and-seek, Gwen?" King's voice yanked her back to reality and cut off whatever Caden was going to say. "Well, ready or not, here I come."

The dog's barks were becoming more frequent and sharper.

"He's heading our way again. We need to move," Caden said.

The tension in his voice was back as he helped her up. Whatever had passed between them was gone now.

"Stay low. We're going to try to outmaneuver him."

They headed in the opposite direction from King, but the undergrowth was getting thicker and keeping their movements quiet was impossible. She bit back a cry as her ankle twisted again, sending another stab up her leg.

I don't know how long I can do this, God.

Ahead of them, sunlight broke through the trees. With no map or knowledge of the terrain, she knew they could be going in circles. Which put them at another disadvantage. King, no doubt, knew this area. They didn't. Another few seconds later, the terrain opened up. Her foot kicked against a small rock that bounced down the slight incline, then off the edge of the canyon that spread out in front of them. Adrenaline punched through her.

"I found you," King shouted. "You lose."

She grabbed Caden's arm, looking for an escape. The canyon edge was in front of them. King and his dog were now behind them and could see them if they went left or right. Panic pressed in harder against her. There was no way out.

"I'm sorry," she said.

"This is not your fault."

If she'd been able to run. If she hadn't had to rely on him to help carry her. He'd been dragged into this situation simply because he'd decided to help her and now...

"I'd stay right there if I were the two of you. Bear will attack if I tell him to, and on top of that my gun is loaded, and I'm a very good shot. The only way out at this point—and I'm sure your minds are scrambling for an escape—would be for the two of you to jump."

King stepped out of the tree line. "Good boy. Bear is a trained search dog. This isn't the first time he's come in handy. I should have known you'd find a way out of that room, but you two just made it to the end of the line, and I wouldn't try anything. Bear might look friendly, but with one word, he's got a mean bite, which means this little game is over."

Caden took a step back with her.

"I'm not sure where you think you're going, but the two of you are more trouble than you're worth. I'm tempted to shoot you both, but fortunately for you, I still need you for a little while longer. So for starters, let's drop that phone you took on the ground."

Caden hesitated, then pulled it out of his pocket and tossed it toward King. Gwen bit the edge of her lip and tried not to cry. Even if his brother had been able to track the phone, chances were they'd never find them now.

King pulled out the battery, then stomped on the phone before throwing it over the edge. "Now, while I might be impressed with your Houdini act and escaping from the safe room, if you intend to get out of this alive, you'll do exactly what I say. Because in case you forgot, we still have an exchange taking place in the next hour. And if you want to ensure any chance of your getting out of here alive… I'd suggest you do exactly what I tell you. Let's go."

Caden's arm tightened around her waist. "She can't walk."

"Oh, I'm sorry." King frowned. "The chauffeur is running behind schedule, along with your afternoon tea."

The dog lunged forward on his leash and growled at them.

Gwen fought the panic. She knew if Caden had been on his own, this scenario would have ended differently. She should have insisted he go on by himself and leave her. King still needed her, so she would be safe, but now, if they left the property, there would be no way for Griffin to find them, even if they had managed to trace the phone before King had destroyed it.

They were on their own from now on.

King stepped in front of her and frowned. "Walk in front of me. Try anything foolish, Gwen, and I will shoot him."

Backtracking to the house was excruciating, but stopping wasn't an option. Ten minutes later, the house loomed in front of them once again. Aaron was out there somewhere with the money waiting for them. She still couldn't believe the situation he'd gotten her into, and yet at the moment, all she wanted was for them all to be safe. But how were they supposed to end this? Her mind refused to stop replaying everything that had happened. Being shoved off the side of the canyon. Caden rescuing her. King shooting Levi, then grabbing her again. It was like a nightmare she couldn't wake up from.

And it wasn't over yet.

King finished binding their hands behind them in the back seat, then secured them with their seat belts.

"Do you have another plan?" Gwen asked Caden as King slammed the back door shut.

"I'd prefer one that works this time," Caden said.

She shot him a wry smile. "Don't give up yet."

He hadn't. Not yet.

In his work in the military, he'd seen firsthand that in situations like this, most perpetrators hadn't intended to end up in the mess they were in, which meant instead of having a formulated plan, they were simply working it out as they went. As far as he was concerned, the only option left was to leave seeds of doubt in the man's mind without making him turn on them, which meant playing on the man's impulsiveness.

Most of what King had done over the past few days had been impulsive, which could work in their favor in the end. Most people who broke the law did so believing firmly that they wouldn't get caught. But leaving a trail of dead bodies behind was taking a huge risk. Unless King somehow found a way to disappear, the authorities would find him and arrest him.

What they needed to do was find a way to keep him off balance.

"So how is this going to play out?" Caden asked as King slipped into the driver's seat. "Exchanges are always tricky with neither party trusting the other."

King's hands gripped the steering wheel. "That's my problem. I've got it all worked out."

"I'm sure you do, and I'm glad, because trust me, I just want this to go as well as you do."

The Jeep flew over a bump in the road, jarring Caden's head against the window as he continued working to loosen the bindings on his wrists, while thinking through his next move. The last thing he wanted to do was make the man angry. He could already tell King was irritated and, more than likely, nervous. And he should be. He'd killed his partner and was now having to make the exchange on his own, which automatically made things more complicated. An exchange in the best of circumstances was risky. Doing it without backup was even riskier. But his gut told him King wasn't looking at the consequences. He simply wanted out of this.

"And when it's over?" Caden asked. "I assume you're planning to leave the country with the money, which would be a good plan considering the body trail you're intending to leave behind."

The muscles in King's jaw tightened. "Sawyer was useless. I only involved him because I needed backup. I never should have let him in."

"The advantage is now you can keep all the money, but I am worried about something else."

King turned onto the main road but didn't respond. Caden decided to keep pressing.

"The problem is that the logistics of disappearing— without getting caught—aren't going to be easy."

"What do you know about disappearing?" King asked.

"I know that disappearing takes time and isn't easy. Not with the digital trails left behind, especially if you plan to stay in the country."

"My plans are none of your business."

"True. I was just thinking how this predicament of yours wasn't planned, but was pretty spur-of-the-moment, which is how you seem to work."

"You know nothing about me."

Caden glanced at Gwen and caught the worry in her eyes, but as far as he was concerned, they had nothing to lose at this point.

"I'm just wondering how much you've really thought this out," Caden said, deciding to continue. "I know you're impulsive, yet motivated. You could rent a small place under an assumed name and get lost in some big city, or you could even vanish and live off the land, but then you'd have to re-create everything about yourself. And you'll always be looking over your shoulder. So I assume you realize that Central or South America is better than staying in the US, because remember you're not just disappearing, you're a fugitive now."

"Law enforcement still doesn't know who I am."

"Maybe not, but they will, and it is true that without Sawyer in the picture, disappearing is going to be a whole lot easier."

The pause from the front seat convinced him he was on the right track.

"I'm right, aren't I?" Caden said. "You knew that this money was your one ticket out of here. It's what made you willing to take the risks you've taken—"

"You know, I've heard enough," King snapped back. "The only thing you need to know is that this exchange will go through, and after that, I'll be long gone."

Caden continued to work on getting his hands free, but he'd learned what he'd wanted to know. King wasn't simply motivated by the money. He was motivated to survive. Quiet engulfed them for the next few minutes as they headed down the main road. Several cars passed them, but there was nothing he could do to get their attention. Frustration multiplied.

"I have a friend who could get you across the border," Gwen said, breaking the silence.

Caden's brow rose at her comment. He had no idea if she was playing the man or was serious, but she'd impressed him by the gutsy move.

"You two don't give up, do you?" King said.

"I figure if I want to ensure we don't end up like Sawyer, we need to make a deal. Unless you already have another plan."

"How does your friend do it? Make a fake passport?"

Caden smiled. The man had taken the bait.

"He's an old friend of mine, and while he hasn't told me much about his...operation, no, you wouldn't need a fake passport."

"Then how?"

"People cross into the US illegally on a daily basis. It's even easier to cross the other way. You use your own passport. He can get you and your money across for a fee. He can even get your passport stamped so you're officially in the country legally."

"And I'm supposed to believe you?"

"She's right. She has as much at stake as you do," Caden said, playing along with her. "We both do."

"It's the perfect deal," Gwen said. "We help you— you let us leave alive."

"And you expect me to trust the two of you?"

Caden's wrists felt raw, but he kept working to undo the rope. Even if King did agree to some kind of deal, there was still no way Caden was going to trust the man to keep his word. He needed to be free in order to put an end to this.

"Probably no more than we trust you," Caden said, "but you have to admit if you're going to get away with this—and whatever else you've done—you need help."

Caden caught King's frown in the rearview mirror.

"Just think about the offer," Gwen said. "You need our help."

"How much farther?" Caden asked.

"Less than an hour."

Caden glanced at Gwen. There was determination in her expression, but he could tell she was worried, too. They might have made their point that King couldn't do this alone, but trusting them…? Well, that was a long shot. Still, while Caden had no idea whether or not Gwen really had the resource she'd claimed to have, he was impressed with her quick thinking. And if all they did was leave serious doubts in King's mind, then that was enough for the moment. They needed him to hesitate over his next move and make a mistake. That was how he was going to get caught.

FOURTEEN

Dark clouds gathered above them an hour later, as King pulled off the main road and headed down a gravel road in the drizzling rain. She could tell that Caden—like herself—was still working to undo the binds behind them, but so far she, at least, hadn't made any progress. Caden had been right about King not following a plan. He was simply acting moment-by-moment and making things up as he went along. She wasn't even sure what his original intentions had been, other than to get his hands on the money and run.

While she hadn't been completely honest about her ability to help King get across the border, it wasn't exactly a lie, either. Samson just wasn't a friend. He was a convicted felon she'd helped send to prison, which was exactly where King needed to be.

A moment later, they came into a clearing where the remains of a few old buildings that had seen better days lined the road ahead of them.

"What is this place?" she asked.

"Looks like an old mining town," Caden said.

Gwen swallowed hard. The place where all of this was going to end one way or another.

She studied what was left of the abandoned log buildings and felt a shiver run through her. A hundred and fifty years ago, this had been a part of the Wild West. A thriving town filled with people convinced they were going to strike it rich. Today it just felt eerie and quiet. No doubt that was what King had wanted. The perfect meeting place for an exchange. Far enough off the main road, where there would be no witnesses, and plenty of places he could dump bodies.

And while she was sure tourists visited, the chances of them coming out in this weather were slim.

King parked about a hundred feet from the first building, then picked up his ringing phone. "Where are you?"

"Coming in from the north." Gwen could hear her brother's answer from the back seat. "I'm two minutes out."

"You better be if you want to see your sister alive. I don't have time to wait."

"Just don't hurt her. Please. I said I'd be there."

"Stop fifty feet from my car, then call me back."

King hung up the call and stepped out of the vehicle, then pulled Gwen out of the back seat. "Don't try anything stupid, unless you want your friend here to die."

She studied King's face as he checked to make sure Caden was still tied securely, but didn't have to ask if he was serious.

We need a way out of this, God, and I don't see one.

"What happens now?" Gwen asked.

King grabbed her arm again, then glanced back at Caden. "You will stay put, and don't try to be the hero, because I promise, you will regret it. I'll have a gun pointed at her the entire time." He squeezed her arm tighter. "As for you, you're going to walk, and get me the cash. You'll make sure it's there, then bring it back here."

Gwen paused. "What guarantee do I have that you won't shoot either of us in the process?"

"I don't exactly owe you any guarantees."

"And after you have the money?" she asked. "You still think you can just walk away from this and no one will find you?"

"What I do isn't any of your business."

Gwen frowned. Except it was. Especially if his business included dumping their bodies.

King pointed his gun on her. "Move now. I want to get this over with."

Ten seconds later, Aaron's car came into sight, driving toward them, and King's phone rang again. "Get out of your vehicle with the money, keeping your hands where I can see them, and walk it halfway," King said. "Drop the money then go back to your car. And don't try anything foolish, or I will shoot your sister."

"Enough with the threats," Aaron said. "I'll do it."

Gwen watched as Aaron stepped out of his car. She wanted to run up to him and ask him what in the world he'd been thinking when he'd stolen the money. How could he have put his own life on the line, as well as hers and the others he'd affected? How could he have been so foolish?

Mostly, though, she just wanted to hug him with relief and for all of this to be over.

But the game King was playing was far from over.

Her brother dropped his phone into his pocket, then grabbed a gym bag out of the car and started slowly toward them.

"That's far enough." King held up his hand when Aaron was halfway between them, then pointed the gun at Gwen. "Walk back to your car and stand in front of it. Gwen, bring the bag back to me."

She started down the gravel road, trying to ignore the pain in her ankle while continuing to pray. She'd never wanted to be the kind of person who only called out to God when things went wrong. She'd always wanted to be the one whose faith was strong enough to believe that no matter what happened, she'd still believe. Like Daniel in the lion's den, or the three men in the fiery furnace. Her faith wouldn't waver.

It wouldn't waver if King killed them.

It wouldn't waver if she lost her brother...

She dug deeper for a thread of faith and held on tight.

"I'm sorry about all of this," Aaron said from where he stood. "Sorry we're not out hiking like we'd planned. Sorry that we're not spending our afternoons sitting at that cabin watching sci-fi marathons."

Sci-fi marathons?

She paused for a second and held her brother's gaze, trying to understand what he wanted her to do. She'd always told him that TV was a distraction when you could be outside enjoying God's creation when they were up here. They'd talked, eaten too much and hiked, but binge-watching? Never.

A distraction.

TV was a distraction.

That was what he wanted.

"Shut up and pick up the money," King shouted.

She reached down and managed to grab the bag despite her hands still zip-tied in front of her, her focus on Aaron.

"Wait…" King said. She turned around and looked back at him. "Hold up what's inside the bag."

She unzipped it slowly, then pulled out a wad of stacked bills.

"Zip it up and get back here now."

Gwen had seen the subtle look Aaron had given her, and prayed he had a plan. Both he and Caden had been trained to handle situations like this and were capable of taking care of themselves. She was the weak link.

But all she needed to give him was a distraction.

She took another step then stumbled, purposely dropping the bag in front of her. "Sorry."

She reached down to pick it back up as King rushed toward her.

"Forget it."

He shifted his attention to the bag. She glanced behind her as Aaron pulled out a handgun. She stepped back, and her brother took a shot.

"What did you just do?" King shouted, stumbling forward.

King tried to grab for Gwen as he dropped to the ground, blood quickly spreading across his shoulder. Caden ran up to her, his hands now free. He kicked away King's gun, then pinned him to the ground with his foot against the man's back.

King groaned in pain.

"Perfect distraction, Gwen," Aaron said as he headed toward them.

"Grab his gun," Caden said.

King groaned again and tried to get up, but Caden shoved the heel of his boot harder into the man's back until he quit struggling. "I said lie down."

Gwen reached for the gun, pausing as the sound of an engine shifted her attention and brought on another surge of adrenaline. A Dodge pulled up beside them, and a man emerged.

"No one move. Leave the gun on the ground." The man trained his gun on them. "I thought I'd find you here, King. And by the way, thanks for taking him down. You're going to make my job so much easier."

"Who are you?" Caden asked.

"The real owner of that bag of money." He took several steps and stood over King. "You didn't really think I was going to let you just walk away."

"I was getting the money for you," King said.

"I'm sure you were."

Aaron started walking toward them again. "You're supposed to be in prison, Anderson."

"And you never should have gotten involved in this."

Aaron kept moving their way.

"That's far enough."

"I was—"

"I said, don't move." Anderson fired a shot. The bullet ripped through the afternoon air.

"No…" She watched her brother stumble forward, a slash of red spreading across his thigh from the bullet. "Aaron?"

Gwen screamed as her brother dropped to the ground.

Caden tried to put the pieces together as Gwen shouted at the man who'd just shot her brother. A light rain had started to fall, but he barely noticed the steady drops.

"Let her go to her brother," Caden said, praying his demand wasn't met with the same result as Aaron's actions.

"Please. I need to stop the bleeding," Gwen begged the man.

Caden caught the panic in Gwen's eyes as Aaron lay motionless. Her face had paled, but he knew how he would have felt if it had been one of his brothers.

"That's all I'll do. I promise," Gwen said. "He needs help."

"Stay where you are and give me the bag."

She hesitated for a moment before grabbing the handle and tossing the bag at him.

Caden took a step back from King, his hands up. He needed to find a way to defuse the situation before someone else got shot. "Let her help him. That's all she wants to do."

The man shifted the gun toward Caden. "Drop to your knees, both of you, and put your hands behind your head."

Caden glanced at Gwen. So this was how it was

going to end. Shot execution-style then buried somewhere out in this vast wilderness?

"You've got this all wrong, Anderson." King managed to sit up, still holding his shoulder where Aaron
had shot him.

"I don't think so. You didn't think you were going
to get away with this, did you? That I would let you
take my money and disappear. You always were impulsive and didn't think things through, but betraying my trust—even I didn't think you were that rash."

"No... I thought you were still in prison. I knew
the money was missing, which is why I'm here...get-
ting your money back." King's fingers pressed into
his shoulder. "You have to believe me."

"And if I hadn't managed to escape during my
transport?" Anderson asked. "Am I to assume you
would have simply kept the money for me?"

"Of course," King said.

"Please...just let me go to him," Gwen interrupted
their conversation.

"Not yet." Anderson unzipped the bag and started
digging through it. "This ridiculous charade you've
been running is over, King."

"I told you—"

"I heard what you told me, but I don't believe you.
I think you'd do anything for three hundred thousand
dollars. Including betray me and anyone else who got
in your way." He zipped up the bag. "Where is Sawyer?"

King ignored the man's stare. "I don't know."

"When I couldn't get ahold of him or you, I assumed you were here together. I'm thinking the two of

you made a deal, but now I'm starting to think Sawyer got the raw end of that deal."

"Sawyer's dead," Caden said. "King shot him back at the house where he was keeping us."

"So you really have made a pretty little mess. You were at my house. Tried to take my money." Anderson leveled his weapon at King. "I should end this now—"

"Please. Don't. I'm telling the truth."

"You betrayed me and killed Sawyer. I have no reason to believe you."

"Sawyer made some bad decisions. I couldn't trust him anymore. But I wouldn't turn on you."

"I think that's exactly what you did." Anderson tossed the bag into the back seat of his car without taking his eyes off them. "Where did you think you were you planning to run to?"

"I wasn't. I was only going to—"

"You know, I really don't care what your plan was." Anderson let out a sharp huff of air, clearly done with King's explanations. He pointed the gun at the man's head. "The problem now is that you've got witnesses that have to be gotten rid of. You really didn't think, did you? You've created a huge mess that I'm going to have to find a way to clean up. Starting with you."

The rain was starting to pick up. Caden caught movement to his right. Gwen's brother was reaching for his gun. A second later he fired off a shot that clipped Anderson's leg.

Reacting automatically, Caden knocked Anderson's gun out of reach as the man stumbled to the ground. Caden grabbed the weapon off the ground and pointed it at Anderson, while Gwen grabbed for King's gun.

"Now it's your turn not to move," Caden shouted at the man. "Move and one of us will shoot you. Drop to your knees now."

Anderson groaned in pain, but obeyed.

The sound of vehicles roared behind them. Caden turned and recognized his brother's squad car. He felt a rush of relief as Griffin and two other officers jumped out of his vehicle.

"It's about time you showed up," Caden said, still holding the gun on the two men, while Gwen ran to her brother.

"Looks to me like you already have everything under control. I just might have to recommend you to my boss. He's been looking at adding another deputy to the team."

"Thanks, but I'm perfectly happy spending my days on the ranch without dealing with situations like this." Caden shot his brother a grin, but couldn't shake just how different this could have ended. "Next time, though, try not to cut it quite so close."

FIFTEEN

Gwen ran to her brother, barely feeling the pain in her ankle thanks to the adrenaline shooting through her. She was still shaking from what had just happened, but she was going to have to take time to process the situation later. No matter how angry she was at her brother for what he'd done, she didn't want anything to happen to him. At least he was alive.

At least they were all alive.

Aaron was trying to get up as she approached him. "I think I'm okay."

"You're not okay." She kneeled down beside him. "You've been shot."

"I'm sorry. All of this was my fault."

"I don't care right now whose fault it is." She pulled off the vest she'd been wearing, folded it once, then pressed it against the wound in an attempt to try to stop the bleeding.

"I never meant for this to happen," Aaron said.

"I know you didn't plan on this, but things like this don't just…happen. You made a decision to cross the line and almost got yourself killed. Almost got me and Caden killed."

"I know." Aaron closed his eyes for a moment. "I don't have any excuses."

"I'm not asking for any." She glanced back. Caden was heading toward them.

"Is he okay?"

"His pulse is a bit fast, but the bleeding seems to have almost stopped."

"Keep up the pressure and hang in there, Aaron. There's an ambulance on the way right now."

Aaron nodded.

Caden squeezed her shoulder. "Are you okay?"

"I will be."

"Stay with him, then. I'll be right back. This is almost over."

Gwen watched Caden walk away, then turned back to her brother. Aaron was in pain. She could tell by the tension radiating down his jaw, but Caden was right. This would all be over soon, but there were still questions she wanted answers to.

"How did this happen?" she asked.

"It's a long story."

She checked his pulse again. "I have a few minutes."

Aaron let out a deep sigh. "I was hired by a bondsman to locate Anderson who'd been involved in drug trafficking. I managed to track him down north of here." He hesitated. "During the arrest, I found a duffel bag in one of the rooms. There was three hundred thousand dollars in cash inside it. And I'm not sure why, but at that moment, I thought I could get away with it. I figured the police wouldn't know anything was missing, and Anderson would think the police had it."

Which unfortunately wasn't what happened. A man was dead. Aaron had been shot...

Aaron grabbed her hand. "You have to believe me when I say that I never meant to get you involved, Gwen. I didn't think anyone else would ever know. But then King and Sawyer went after the money, and Anderson managed to escape... At the very least I'm going to lose my license. I'll probably end up in prison, as well. I'm just... I'm so, so sorry."

She stuffed back her frustration.

She was sorry, too. Sorry for the entire situation he'd roped her into. Sorry she'd had to spend the past two days fighting to stay alive. But she also knew that her brother needed grace right now more than anything else.

Two ambulances pulled up behind the squad cars.

"Forget about all of that right now. We're going to get through this," she said. "The paramedics are here."

The next few minutes were a blur. Someone told her to move out of the way so they could help her brother. She nodded, then stumbled backward as a sharp pain shot through her leg. But it didn't matter. She was safe. She just had to keep reminding herself of that, because she didn't feel safe. She glanced down at her hands, which were covered with her brother's blood, and the fear and panic struck all over again.

She stepped aside while a whirl of activity continued around her, and tried to process everything. Paramedics worked on the gunshot wounds. Caden spoke to his brother and another officer. After a few minutes, one of the paramedics came with wet wipes and helped clean the blood off her hands, then started to check her ankle.

Caden walked over. "I asked him to check on your ankle."

"Thank you," she said.

"We'll do X-rays at the hospital," the man said as he finished up. "But it looks like it's just badly sprained."

"My nerves, on the other hand…" She waited for the paramedic to walk away. "Tell me this is finally over. Please."

"Anderson and King are in custody. Plus, they think they've found the house where we were held. They'll start searching for Sawyer's body there."

"It still all seems too surreal."

"I know." He pulled her into his arms and let her lean against him. "You're so cold."

He took off his jacket and wrapped it around her shoulders. "What are you thinking?"

"I'm just still trying to wrap my mind around what happened. And I'm worried about my brother. He told me briefly about what happened, but the truth is that no matter how glad I am that he's okay, I'm still angry at him."

"That's understandable. He's going to have to face the consequences."

"I know." She managed a smile. "On the bright side, you saved my life. Again."

"Your brother did help with that."

She caught his gaze and felt her heart stir at his nearness. How had this happened? They'd somehow gone from sworn enemies to her suddenly wanting to kiss him very, very badly.

* * *

Caden tried to read Gwen's expression as her lips parted, and she seemed to study his face. Something inside him shifted, pulling him to a place he wasn't sure he wanted to go. And yet he didn't know how much longer he could ignore what he was feeling toward her.

"He wasn't going to let us live," she said finally, breaking the silence between them. "Neither of them could have. I can't stop thinking of what almost happened."

"I know, but we don't have to worry about them anymore. We're safe, this is over, and like Griffin said, those men are going away for a long, long time."

She nodded, but he knew what she was thinking. For her and Aaron, this wasn't over. Not yet. The authorities were going to arrest Aaron for his part in all of this. But despite what her brother had done and the downward spiral of everything in the wake of his bad decisions, at least they were alive.

Still, the irony of the situation wasn't lost on him. He'd thought he would be perfectly content to never see the woman again, and yet they'd just spent the past forty-eight hours together proving everything he'd thought about her completely wrong.

"Caden, there's something I need to tell you. I…"

She paused as she looked up at him, but instead of finishing her sentence, she slid her arms around his neck and kissed him on the lips, taking him completely off guard. His mind spun and his heart raced as he automatically kissed her back. She felt warm against him, inviting, as he savored the discovery of the unexpected kiss. He hadn't been able to admit it to himself, but this—this was what he'd wanted.

"I'm sorry." She pulled away from him suddenly and dropped her hands to her sides. "This situation has messed with my emotions."

"It's okay." He stumbled with his words. "This *has* been emotional. For both of us."

"But I should never have kissed you. I've just been so scared, and now I'm worried about my brother... Honestly, I have no idea what came over me. You've been this rock for me the past few days, but I never should have turned it into something romantic."

His mind tried to work through his own feelings. Falling for Gwen had never been on his agenda. He'd just done what he'd known to be right.

"It's okay. We can talk about this later, but for now we need to get you to the hospital and get your foot X-rayed."

She nodded, but he couldn't ignore what had just passed between them with that kiss. Or that the past few days had twisted his heart, making him feel for the first time in a very long time that he just might want to take a chance on love again. It seemed ridiculous on the surface, and yet he also knew that Gwen wasn't the woman he'd thought she was. Instead, there was something about her he wasn't sure he was going to be able to shake.

She looked up at him, her eyes still wide. "So we're okay?"

He brushed the back of his hand against his lips, still feeling the intensity of her touch. "We are."

"I'm sorry to interrupt." Griffin came up beside him. "But we're about ready to leave."

"We're ready." Caden stepped back, even more uncomfortable, and wondered how much his brother had seen. More than likely he'd witnessed the kiss, and if he had, Caden would never hear the end of it. "Gwen, this is one of my brothers, Griffin. I think the two of you might have met back in college."

"I think we did," Griffin said. "It's nice to see you again, though these aren't exactly the conditions anyone hopes for."

The softness Gwen had in her eyes when she'd looked at him earlier was gone. "It's been a rough few days."

"I'm just glad that the two of you are okay."

"Me, too. Is there an immediate plan?" she asked.

"As soon as the doctor releases him, he'll be escorted to the courthouse for his arraignment. There's no way to know if he'll be allowed to post bail. If he cooperates, it will help. Beyond that, I really can't tell you much more at this point."

"I understand. Thank you." She glanced briefly at Caden. "What about Anderson and King?"

"From what I heard, they were pretty intent on taking each other down. What I do know is that they'll be going away for a long, long time."

Gwen took another step back. "Do you think they'll let me ride with my brother in the ambulance?"

"You can ask them, but I'm sure they'll let you."

"She does need to see a doctor, as well. Her ankle's pretty messed up."

"We'll make sure someone sees her as soon as we get back to town."

"Thank you," Gwen said.

"I'll catch up with you in a minute," Caden said to Gwen, then waited for her to leave before turning back to his brother. "Go ahead. I know you're dying to ask what's going on."

Griffin grinned at him. "I do have some catching up to do. I mean, it isn't often that you go camping on a solo weekend and come home with a beautiful woman."

"Very funny. She was just saying thank-you for saving her life."

"Really? It's just that's a pretty intimate way of saying thank-you."

"It's been an emotional few days, but I don't think anything will come of it. She'll be heading back to Denver as soon as this is over. I'll be back at the ranch…"

"You didn't exactly seem to be running in the other direction. In fact, from where I was standing it looked as if you were a willing participant."

"You're not going to let this drop, are you?"

"Nope."

"Enough. I knew her a long time ago. She was Cammie's best friend."

"Wait a minute… Your ex-fiancée, Cammie?"

Caden nodded.

"Okay, I'm definitely missing something here."

"There's nothing going on between us. Not really. Besides, even if there were, I wouldn't be too quick to judge. Who would have imagined you'd marry a girl you met while playing bodyguard for the FBI?"

"Touché, but still…once we get you home, you're going to need to catch me up on all the details."

"Like I said, there's nothing."

"You never know. Denver's not that far away—"

Caden started back toward the vehicles, with Griffin following him. "Don't even go there."

"I'll stop if you just promise me you won't close off your heart because of fear."

He dismissed his brother's advice. "I'm not afraid of falling in love again."

Griffin put his hand on his brother's shoulder and moved in front of him. "Then maybe it's finally time to give it a try."

SIXTEEN

She couldn't believe she'd kissed him.

Gwen stepped out of the exam room after seeing the doctor with a dozen things running through her mind. Gratefulness that her ankle wasn't broken. Worry about her brother's surgery. Fear over what was going to happen to him... But there was another thing she couldn't shake. What in the world had she been thinking when she kissed Caden O'Callaghan?

The confusion she felt had followed her all the way to Timber Falls, and still wouldn't leave her alone, because she had no idea what had overcome her. She was right to tell him how thankful she was to him for risking his life to save her, but that was where things should have ended. She'd acted completely out of emotion, not reality.

Reality was that her brother had committed a felony and it would take everything she had to help him get through the foreseeable future. Reality was that no matter who Caden was today, she'd watched him break her best friend's heart, something that was hard to forget.

"Gwen…"

She stopped in the middle of the hallway and turned around. Caden was coming toward her, concern written across his expression. She let her gaze linger on him for a few seconds too long. From his cowboy hat to those piercing gray-blue eyes of his that always seemed to see right into her heart, to the stubbled beard that had grown over the past few days. She swallowed hard. No. She'd been right to stop anything before it got started. The last thing she wanted to do was lead her heart into dangerous territory, and that was exactly where she was heading if she wasn't careful.

"They told me I'd find you here," Caden said. "What did the doctor say?"

She pushed aside her tremulous thoughts and pointed to her walking boot. "I get to wear this for the next few weeks. The good news, though, is that the doctor said it isn't broken, and that it will heal completely. I just need to stay away from things like running marathons and hiking canyons the next few weeks."

"That's some pretty sound advice, I'd say."

He caught her gaze, and her stomach fluttered, while awkwardness settled between them.

All because of one kiss.

"Listen, I'm sorry about what happened earlier today." She plowed forward with her excuses, needing to clear the air between them. "I was completely out of line and have no idea what came over me. I never, ever go around kissing men unsolicited, even when they save my life. Bottom line is that I guess all of this…is just uncharted territory for me, and I'm feeling a bit lost and vulnerable."

He slipped his thumbs into the back pockets of his jeans. "What if that kiss wasn't completely unwanted?"

Her eyes widened at his response.

"I just meant… I just meant that kissing you wasn't…well, it wasn't exactly offensive," he said. "But if you'd like, we can forget it ever happened."

Oh, yeah. She really needed to forget that kiss, because she had no intentions of putting her heart on the line again.

"I think that's best," she said. "Because—"

"You don't have to explain." Caden cleared his throat. "We can just leave it at that."

"I think we should."

"Bruce and Levi are here, along with Bruce's wife, Alisha, and Levi's fiancée, Kennedy. They'd like to meet us."

"Okay." She blew out a breath, thankful for the change in subject. "Maybe we should pick up something for them at the gift shop."

"A peace offering?" Caden asked.

Gwen forced a laugh. "Something like that."

Five minutes later, they were making introductions in the middle of room 312, where Levi was lying in bed, recovering after his surgery.

Gwen held out the boxes of chocolates she and Caden had bought. "We heard you're a bit of a chocolate snob."

Bruce's eyes brightened. "You didn't."

"A friend of mine here in town makes these," Caden said. "They sell them at the gift shop. Best chocolate you'll ever taste."

"We've heard about these," Levi said. "And have

always talked about picking some up. They're supposed to be amazing."

"They are," Caden said. "And while it won't make up for getting shot, we hope you enjoy them."

Levi shot them a smile. "I have a feeling these will ease the pain."

Gwen shoved her hands into her pockets. "I just want to say how sorry we are about everything. When we flagged down your raft, we had no idea just how bad everything was going to get."

Kennedy squeezed Levi's hand from the side of the bed where he was resting. "I'll admit that the initial phone call had me in a panic, but honestly, both these guys would never simply walk away from trouble. And on the plus side, according to the local news, they're heroes. Though I already knew that. I'd trust these guys with my life any day."

Trusted them with her life.

The words dug through her, as she tried to shake the conflicting emotions between wanting to give Caden a chance and running.

"Bottom line is that we owe you both our lives," Caden said.

"What about your brother?" Bruce asked. "How is he?"

"He's in surgery right now," Gwen said, "but the doctors are optimistic."

One of the nurses walked in, clearly unhappy about the crowded room and her patient who, according to her, was supposed to be resting.

"We were just heading out." Caden pressed his hand

against the small of Gwen's back as they took a step back. "But thank you. All of you."

"I'm guessing you want to go see about your brother," Caden said as they left the room.

Gwen nodded. "He should be getting out of surgery soon."

"Would you like me to wait with you?"

"Do you mind?"

"Of course not."

A part of her felt relieved as they started walking down the hallway, that she wasn't going to have to wait alone. But on the other hand, she'd answered before she had time to weigh her response. Why couldn't her heart listen to her head?

Caden's phone rang, and he pulled it out of his pocket. "It's my mom."

"Talk to her. I'll be fine."

"I know, but I'll be right there."

The surgical waiting room was on the second floor of the small hospital, which was decorated in blues and grays with calming artwork on the walls. But she wasn't sure anything could calm her spirit at this point. She'd only just sat down and pulled out her phone, when a woman wearing purple scrubs and a bright smile walked up to her. "You wouldn't be Gwen Ryland by any chance, would you?"

"I am."

"I'm Tory Faraday. Caden's brother Griffin's fiancée"

"Hi. It's nice to meet you."

The woman's smile widened as she sat down next to Gwen. "I was looking for you because not only did

I want to meet you, but also because I assisted with your brother's surgery and heard you were here."

Gwen's hands fisted at her sides as the anxiety struck again. "Please tell me he's okay."

"The surgeon was able to take out the bullet and repair most of the damaged tissue."

"And his recovery?"

"There will more than likely be some nerve damage, but we're optimistic he'll get back most of his shoulder movement. In the meantime, you'll be able to see him in about thirty minutes."

Gwen pressed her hand against her chest. "I'm so happy to hear that. These past few days have been pretty stressful."

Tory glanced down at Gwen's boot. "Are you okay?"

"The doctor said it just needs a few weeks to heal." The pain medicine the nurse had given her was starting to kick in, but at the moment, she'd rather forget the reminder. "When are you getting married?"

Tory held up her hand to show Gwen her engagement ring. "Four more months. I keep pinching myself to remind me it's real."

"I'm happy for you."

"Thank you, but I'm sorry about this. How are you? It's been quite a nightmare from what I've heard."

"I think a part of me still thinks I'm going to wake up. The other part is just eternally grateful that I'm still alive. Honestly, I don't think the realness has completely hit yet."

"There is something about an experience like this that will change your life forever." Tory fiddled with the ring on her finger. "You don't know my story, but someone wanting to take your life is terrifying. I can attest to that firsthand. Right now I'm just doing my best to put it all behind me. It's hard, I know, but don't be afraid to talk with someone, get some counseling or see your pastor. Or if you ever want to grab coffee sometime, I'd love to do that. I'm living here now."

Gwen nodded. "Maybe I'll get a chance to hear your story one day, but thank you. I really appreciate it." She felt her shoulders relax some, realizing there was something cathartic about talking to someone who understood. "I know you're right. And I will. At this point, though, I feel like my entire life has been ripped apart. My brother…he's really my only family, and if he goes to prison…"

"Mistakes of others can be difficult when you have to live with the consequences. I understand that. And while the pain won't necessarily completely disappear, it will get easier. Just be there for him. That's what he needs right now. And take time to care for yourself, as well."

"Thank you. I'm going to try." Gwen pushed back the tears that threatened to spill out. "So what's it like being a part of the O'Callaghan family?"

Tory laughed. "I'm learning there's never a dull minute, but I can't imagine not being a part of their lives. What about you and Caden? I heard the two of you go way back."

Gwen forced a smile, but really didn't want to go into her relationship with Caden. "I guess you could call us old friends, but *acquaintances* is probably more the right word. We haven't seen each other for years."

"Maybe not, but he sure went the extra mile for an old friend."

"He did, but there isn't anything between us. Romantically, anyway."

Then why did you kiss him?

"He's a wonderful guy," Tory said, not seeming to catch Gwen's conflicting emotions. "I'm always amazed at how good he is with the horses and running the ranch."

"I'm not surprised."

"And I think he needs a good woman in his life. I've heard enough of what happened to you to know you had to be strong to go through what you just did."

Gwen glanced at the doorway of the waiting room, suddenly feeling uncomfortable.

"I'm sorry." Tory laid her hand on Gwen's arm for a moment, then stood up. "I shouldn't have said that. When I first started getting to know the O'Callaghan family, it was pretty overwhelming because I come from a small family. But there's so much love and acceptance there. I can't imagine not having them in my life."

"I'm happy for you, but as for Caden and me... I meant what I said. There's nothing between us other than the fact that I'll always be grateful to him for rescuing me." Gwen blinked back the tears. "Congratulations again."

"Thank you. I appreciate it. And, Gwen? You already know this, but Caden is a great guy."

Gwen frowned. Maybe. But she also knew that with Caden there was too big a risk of her ending up with a broken heart.

* * *

Caden hurried toward the waiting room, trying to come up with what he was going to say to Gwen. He'd thought the past couple days had erased the years of mistrust they'd held toward each other. Thought that maybe theirs was a relationship worth pursuing. But apparently he was wrong, because she clearly didn't feel the same way.

A minute later, he paused in the doorway of the sitting room where she was sitting on one of the chairs, typing something on her phone. He hadn't wanted his heart to stir every time he saw her. And it wasn't just the connection he felt because of everything that had happened to them. She made him laugh. Made him wonder what it would be like to take a risk with his heart again. He could see them working together on his ranch, using the facilities for trauma victims and veterans…but that was never going to happen.

Maybe it was simply that Liam and Griffin, who'd managed to fall in love recently, had made him feel like he was missing something—or rather, someone—in his life. But whatever the reason, it really didn't matter. He'd tell her goodbye and never see her again. That was the reality.

"Caden…" She looked up at him and smiled. "I didn't see you. I was letting some of my friends know what was going on. Asking them to pray."

"That's good. And I'm sorry about the phone call. I hadn't been able to connect with my parents until now. As you can imagine, they've been worried sick."

"I'm sure they have. I'm glad you talked to them."

"They're on their way here now, but what about you? Any news on your brother?"

"Yes, actually." She slipped her phone into her back pocket. "I just talked to your future sister-in-law, Tory, who assisted with his surgery. The doctor is pleased and believes he'll make a full recovery. I should be able to go in and see him soon."

"That's great. I'm glad to hear that."

"Me, too, but then he'll end up in prison, and—"

"Don't think about that right now." He sat down next to her. "Just concentrate on him getting better. One thing at a time."

"I know—it's just hard."

He studied the pattern on the carpeted floor, wishing he knew what to say to help her feel better. But he also knew that this wasn't a situation he could fix.

"So you met Tory," he said, searching for something to say.

"Yeah…she seems good for your brother."

"She is."

And you—you seem so good for me.

"I know this is all hard on you," he said.

"I won't try to pretend I'm not frustrated. I thought Aaron had finally gotten to a place in his life where he was beyond doing something like this, but this choice of his…" She shook her head. "He's made such a mess of things. I had to call his boss…and his girlfriend. She's on her way here now."

"What were their reactions?"

"His boss is understandably furious. And Emma… I don't think she knew how to react. She was pretty taken aback by everything that happened. And I don't blame her. I don't know how to handle this, either."

He pressed his hands together, praying God would give him the right words that would somehow encourage her.

"I think you have to remember that while this situation with your brother probably seems insurmountable, there's a bigger picture we can't see. God can still redeem this."

"I know."

But even though she said the words, she didn't look convinced.

"I'm not trying to sound cliché—"

"You're not." She looked up at him. "It's just that while I'm praying for exactly that, I still feel so out of control."

"I've always had a hard time believing that everything happens for a reason, but I do believe God can redeem this situation. People make bad decisions. Think of King David, Moses and Jonah. And, yes, there are consequences that are going to play out, and he's going to need to take responsibility for that, but don't let this choice of his become all you see."

"I will try."

"It probably won't be easy, but the bottom line is that God designed us to be reliant on Him. Don't try to do this on your own."

"People tend to seek God when things are falling apart. I just… I've tried to be the anchor in my brother's life—"

"You've tried to handle it all on your own."

She shot him a sliver of a smile. "Most of the time, I supposed I have."

"Just remember you're not alone. In fact, my parents wanted me to ask if you'd like to come out to the ranch for a few days while you wait for him to recover. It's not that far away, and it would be quiet. I could even show you some of my favorite places. We could ride some horses…or you could use the time to be alone. Whatever you want. After all that's happened, I'd say you deserve a few days of quiet."

"I appreciate it. I really do, but I think I need to stay here in town, close to my brother. At least until they take him into custody. I called one of the local B and Bs while I was waiting for the doctor to see me, and I have a room for the next few nights."

"Okay. That's fine… I understand."

He shoved away his disappointment. At least his head understood. His heart wanted her to trust him.

"And you don't have to wait with me." She glanced at her watch and stood up. "I think they'll let me see him now."

He felt the wall back up between them, wishing now she'd never kissed him, while at the same time wishing desperately he could kiss her again.

"If you change your mind, just call," he said. "You have my number. And if you need anything—anything at all—call me."

"I will, and thank you."

"And Gwen. I just…" He searched for what to say before she walked out of the room. "After everything we went through, I don't want to leave with things sour between us."

All because of a kiss.

"I don't, either, and please know that I will forever be grateful for what you did for me."

But clearly nothing more.

He watched her walk away a moment later, wishing he didn't feel that continuous tug of his heart when he was around her. Maybe she was right, and he could never be that person in her life. Because no matter what had happened between them, she wasn't ever going to forget what had taken place all those years ago. And really, he couldn't blame her. Of course, if things had been different back then... If she'd known the truth... He shook off the thought. None of that mattered anymore. She needed to focus on getting her brother through the next few weeks, and he needed to forget her. Because while she might have trusted him with her life, she clearly wasn't going to trust him with her heart.

SEVENTEEN

Two months later

Gwen sat at one of the booths in the back of the restaurant waiting for Cammie to arrive, but her mind was struggling to focus. She'd been surprised to hear her friend was back in town. It seemed strange to be meeting for lunch with Cammie when she'd just received an invitation from Caden's parents for the Fourth of July, an invitation she'd yet to respond to, because there was still something holding her back from going.

Caden.

Which made no sense.

Didn't she want to see him?

Despite her conflicted feelings, they'd texted and called each other regularly over the past few weeks, and she'd found herself getting to know the man she'd resented so much over the past decade. And the result had been surprising. She'd found herself reaching for her phone far too often just to see how his day was going, or to get his advice on something. On top of that, she'd shared more with him about her desire to start a wilderness expedition program, while dreaming about him at night and waking up wanting to talk to him.

But the whole time they'd just skirted around the idea of a relationship between them, and she knew it was her fault. Because every time she thought about moving forward with him, she couldn't stop thinking that she was headed for inevitable heartache. Maybe Caden really was trustworthy, but Seth had broken her heart, and made her afraid to give it away again.

On the other hand, while he might not be the man she once thought he was, that didn't mean he was falling for her. He'd been honest with his input for her ideas on her wilderness trek, even to the point of considering expanding what he was doing at the ranch, but it wasn't as if that was a marriage proposal. And she wasn't looking for a business partner.

But neither could she shake the question of how the man she'd thought was so self-centered and egotistical had turned into someone who was managing to steal her heart. He might have changed, but what if what had happened to Cammie happened to her?

"Gwen?" Cammie waved at her as she approached. "There you are. So sorry I'm late."

Gwen slid out of the booth and gave her friend a hug. "I'm so glad to see you."

"You were a million miles away."

"Sorry." She shot her friend a smile. Cammie had changed little over the years, from the cute outfit she'd probably picked up at the boutique downtown, to the perfect mani and pedi, and eyelashes that were a mile long... "I was just thinking."

"I'm just glad to see you're all right." Cammie slid into the booth. "How's your brother? When I saw the story about him on the news, I had to see you. You must be horrified."

Gwen frowned, not missing the hint of scandal in her friend's voice. "He's currently out on bail, which is ironic for a bounty hunter. His court case has just been scheduled for September. More than likely he'll end up facing some jail time."

Saying it out loud made it seem even more real, but it was what it was. He'd made bad choices and, like it or not, he was going to have to live with the consequences.

"I have to imagine it's pretty stressful," Cammie said, clearly digging for details.

"It is."

The waitress came over, and Cammie asked for a glass of ice water with lime, not lemon. "I told my mother what had happened, and she was shocked. She met your brother at least once and couldn't believe he was involved in the scandal."

Cammie waved her hands while she rambled on, leaning in for emphasis every few seconds. It was like they were back in college, but while Gwen had grown beyond the need to dig up the latest gossip, she wasn't sure Cammie ever had. Funny how it wasn't even Cammie's brother who'd been arrested, and yet her friend was still was managing to be the center of attention.

"Do you have plans for the Fourth?" Cammie asked, barely taking a breath before sipping on the water their waitress had brought her.

Gwen worked to keep her expression neutral. "I was invited somewhere for the weekend, but I don't think I'm going."

"Who's the invitation from?"

"Just some friends. A family who lives south of here on a ranch."

"I bet it's beautiful."

"It is," Gwen said, wanting to change the subject before it switched to Caden. "Tell me—"

"I'd love to tag along if I didn't have to get back to my family."

"You have a great family."

"I thought I had a great family." Cammie's smile faded. "Jeff and I are getting a divorce. That's one of the reasons I'm back in town. I needed to get away."

"What?"

"It's a long time coming, though I never thought it would really happen. Turns out we want completely different things. Have different goals."

"I'm really sorry to hear that." The confession surprised her. She'd thought—at least from the outside—that their relationship had been good. Apparently, she'd been wrong.

"Me, too."

Gwen swirled the straw in her tea and frowned. No one was perfect—she had no illusions about that—but it was still sad. She'd always looked at marriage as forever, if at all possible.

"Jeff's keeping the kids right now, but you can imagine how awkward it has been."

"I really am sorry."

"Forget about me and my drama… What about you? Are you dating anyone?"

"No."

Cammie cocked her head. "You're hiding something from me."

Gwen frowned. Even if they had been dating, Caden wasn't exactly a subject she was going to bring up.

"Don't be ridiculous."

"I'm hardly being ridiculous. You've got that dreamy, head-in-the-clouds look written all over you. Who is it?"

She signaled for the waitress. "No one."

Which was true. She wasn't in love with Caden. Just because he was handsome, charming and nothing like the man she'd believed he was didn't mean there was anything between them.

The waitress stepped up to their table to take their orders.

"I'll have the Cobb salad, please." Gwen handed the woman her menu, hoping the distraction had ended their conversation.

"Sounds delicious. I'll have the same thing." Cammie took another sip of her water, then set it down in front of her. "I was shocked to hear that Caden was somehow involved in what happened with your brother."

"He was out camping." Gwen tried to keep her voice steady. Clearly this was the real reason for the impromptu lunch. "He ended up saving my life."

"That's so crazy. How is he?"

"He's doing well."

"You must have talked with him some."

"Of course. He's—he's working his father's ranch."

Cammie's eyes widened as she put the pieces together. "Your plans for the Fourth."

So much for her plans not to talk about Caden.

"My potential plans for the Fourth."

"And why wouldn't you want to go?"

"Because…"

Because she couldn't move forward until she knew what really happened that night.

"Can I ask you a question?" Gwen asked.

"Of course."

"What really happened the night you and Caden broke things off?"

She knew she was stepping on rocky ground, but even if there was no future between her and Caden, she needed to know the truth.

"That was a long time ago, Gwen. If he's the one you're interested in and you're worried about my reaction, you don't have to be, though I certainly hope he's changed. We had issues. Both of us. And I—I admit, I had been questioning things for weeks before the wedding."

"Did he really break things off with you?"

Cammie grabbed the napkin off the table and squeezed it. "I made some mistakes. In less than twenty-four hours all the guests were going to arrive. Canceling the wedding would have ruined everything, I just… I didn't know what to do."

"So you blamed him."

"Gwen…"

"I just need to know the truth."

Friends and family had rallied around her. But if

that was nothing more than a lie? She tried to shake the next thought, but it wouldn't disappear.

"Were you in love with Jeff while engaged to Caden?"

"Gwen…that was years ago. None of that matters anymore."

"It matters to me."

"Why?"

"It just…does."

"Fine. Caden was busy with school and work, and I was lonely. I never meant anything by it. Jeff and I just started going out as friends. Sometimes a movie. Sometimes dinner."

"You were engaged to Caden. He trusted you."

"I made mistakes. And now it turns out I chose the wrong man again."

"But you always told me he broke things off and broke your heart. That he was the love of your life and he'd betrayed you." A seed of frustration and anger sprouted. "I talked to him that night. Told him exactly what I thought about his behavior, and I wasn't very nice."

Cammie shrugged. "What did you expect me to do? Tell my guests that I'd cheated on my fiancé? How would that have made me look?"

Gwen couldn't believe what she was hearing. "He never told anyone, Cammie. He let everyone there that night believe that it was his fault. He took all the blame because no matter what you did, he still loved you."

"Why does any of that matter? Because you're in love with him, aren't you? He played the hero and rescued you and now you've fallen for him."

"I'm not in love with him."

Gwen stared at Cammie's necklace, then dropped her gaze. She never should have agreed to meet with her. She'd heard enough now to know that everything Caden had told her was true. And everything Cammie had told her was nothing more than lies.

"You are, aren't you?"

"I never said I was in love with him. His parents invited me to the ranch, actually. They're just being nice. They know I've been having a hard time with my brother and thought I could use a weekend away."

"It's just hard to imagine my best friend falling for my ex-fiancé. I'm not sure I can wrap my mind around that."

"He used to be good enough for you."

"That wasn't exactly what I meant. I have no interest in a relationship with Caden, and if you want my blessing, you have it. That was a long time ago and I'm certainly not the same person. I'm sure he's not, either. The two of you are probably perfect for each other, anyway. As far as I'm concerned, you can have Caden O'Callaghan and his stuffy morals."

"Cammie, I—"

The waitress stopped in front of their table and set the salads in front of them.

"You know what?" Cammie stood up and grabbed her bag. "I'm not hungry anymore."

Gwen's heart pounded as she watched Cammie stomp away. How had she been so wrong about someone? About both Cammie *and* Caden?

Caden was at the main house when he heard a car coming down the gravel road. He stepped out onto the porch, feeling the pack of nerves he'd tried to stuff down all morning shoot up again. When Gwen had accepted his parents' invitation for the Fourth of July weekend, he'd panicked at the thought of her visiting.

Which didn't make sense.

He'd enjoyed their frequent conversations over the past few weeks, and felt like every time they spoke, he got to know her a little better. They'd spent time talking about everything from their dislikes, to quirks, to deeper things like faith and their values. And the more he'd learned about her, the more he'd realized they were on the same page. But nothing they'd said on the phone, or via texting, had crossed the line from friendship toward something more. And that was the problem. Every time he'd tried to move their relationship forward, he felt her holding back. But maybe he shouldn't be surprised. He wanted a relationship with the woman who'd despised him for over a decade.

The bottom line was he was thirty-two and had lived enough to know exactly what he wanted. And Gwen was what he wanted—but she had no feelings for him.

He met her car, opened up her door and felt a familiar stir as she slid out of the driver's seat and smiled up at him.

"I'm glad you came." He pulled her into a hug, resisting the urge to kiss her as he took in her red sundress, perfect for the patriotic weekend. "You look great."

He swallowed hard. *She* was perfect for him.

"Thanks. There was a conflict at work, and I wasn't

sure I was going to be able to come for a while, but I managed to sort things out and get away."

"I'm glad." He studied those wide blue eyes of hers and wondered how he could have missed her so much. "My mother's got the guest room ready for you, so you can make yourself at home for the weekend."

She shoved her keys into her pocket. "I really could have driven back to Denver tonight. I don't want to be any trouble."

"You're no trouble. Trust me. My mom loves having the house full. The more family and friends around, the happier she is."

"I hope so." She pulled out a pink carry-on suitcase from the back seat and set it on the ground.

"Is there more in the back?" he asked.

"No. I'm a pretty light packer."

"I'm impressed. I've seen my mother take three times this much for just an overnight trip." He stopped in front of her. "Before we go in…how are you? I know that the past few weeks have been hard."

A shadow crossed her face. "It has been tough. I know Aaron will spend some time in jail and lose his bounty-hunter license, but at least he's alive. I keep telling myself that God gives second chances, and I need to be there for him."

"You're not alone in this." He glanced at her sandals. "What about your ankle?"

"It's finally healed, thankfully."

"I'm glad to hear that, as well."

She looked toward the house. "Where is everybody?"

"My mom's still here, but Mia wanted to go see the

cows, so everyone took the Jeep out to the west pasture to check on them."

"Mia's Gabby and Liam's child?"

Caden nodded. "She's two and has completely stolen everyone's hearts."

"Caden?"

His mother hurried toward the car, waving at them. "I guess I'm not the only one excited to see you."

Without even hesitating, his mother stopped in front of them and pulled Gwen into a hug. "I'm so glad you decided to come."

"I appreciate the invitation, though I was surprised."

"You shouldn't be. We've been wanting to meet you. It's become a bit of a family reunion with all my boys here, plus current and future daughters-in-law, and a grandbaby… I'm sure you'll fit right in once you meet everyone."

Gwen glanced up at him. "I still think that if I lived here all I'd do is sit on the front porch and enjoy the view."

Caden smiled at the soft blush crossing her cheeks. Maybe she felt somewhat presumptuous by her statement, but he loved the thought of the two of them spending hours on the front porch together.

"Honestly, I never get tired of the view," his mom said. "And you can sit all you want on the porch. Let me take your bag up to the house. Lunch isn't going to be ready for another hour, so Caden, why don't the two of you go for a walk before everyone gets back. The weather's perfect."

"I'd be happy to come inside and help with lunch," Gwen said.

"You didn't come here to work—"

"I would like to show you around a bit," Caden said. Knowing his family, this might be the only time he got to be alone with her.

The sound of tires on the gravel interrupted his thoughts as the Jeep pulled up in front of Gwen's car. Caden frowned. Too late.

He forced a smile as his family piled out of the Jeep and he started making introductions. "Gwen, this is my youngest brother, Liam, and his wife, Gabby, and, of course, Mia."

"I hear you're expecting another little one. Congratulations," Gwen said.

Gabby beamed. "Thank you."

"We're superexcited," Liam said. "And it's great to meet you."

"You've already met Griffin and Tory. Reid's the only one not here, besides my father, and they should both be back soon."

"Nice to meet all of you. I've been looking forward to this weekend."

He put his hand on Gwen's arm, not wanting to miss a few minutes alone with her. "Why don't you all head up to the house. I'm going to show Gwen around a bit before lunch."

Laughter and chatting faded as the group headed to the house and he turned back to her. "Sorry about that. When my entire family gets together it can be a bit overwhelming."

"No, it's fine. Really. I've been looking forward to meeting your family. They're all so nice and welcoming."

"Good, because I really am glad you're here."

They headed down a tree-lined path that led to the pond. He drew in a deep breath of fresh air, surprised at how much he'd missed her. And how glad he was that she was here with him.

"I've been talking to my father about your idea, as you know," he said as they walked. "He's really interested in bringing corporations and local businesses on board. I'd like your input, but we're thinking about implementing some of your ideas. I'd like to also have a free program for veterans."

"I love that idea."

"I thought you would. There's a lot more that we'd have to talk about, but I've definitely been doing a lot of thinking about it." *Been thinking a lot about you.* "I'd love your thoughts on making the idea a reality."

Doubts from his practical side shot through him as he tried to read her expression.

Just tell her how you really feel before you go any further.

"Gwen, I—"

"I'd love to brainstorm with you and your father, but there's something I really need to talk to you about first."

"Of course."

She turned toward him. The mountains framed her in the background, making him want to snap a photo and preserve the moment.

"I don't know how else to say it than just jumping into it," she said. "I saw Cammie a few days ago. She called me up out of the blue and wanted to go out to lunch. Apparently she'd seen a newspaper article about us and my brother, and the entire fiasco, and had to know more."

"Cammie?" His ex-fiancée wasn't exactly the topic of conversation he'd expected. "Okay...how is she?"

"Getting a divorce. I was pretty surprised to hear that, but there was something else I was even more surprised about. Why didn't you tell me the truth about her? That she cheated on you and you turned around and let her lie about you. Even when I confronted you, you never said anything. Why?"

"Back then... I suppose because I still loved her and didn't see the point in ruining her reputation."

"She didn't have any trouble trying to ruin yours."

He stuffed his hands in his pockets, not sure where this was going. "That night I was hurt, understandably. But when she started telling everyone how I'd broken up with her, I realized that I could have married her and found out later who she really was. I was simply grateful that didn't happen, even though it was painful to find out that way."

"I have to say I admire you for not trashing her reputation, because she deserved it."

How was he supposed to respond?

"Cammie had this charm about her that had me blinded. In the back of my mind, I told myself I could put up with her faults, because there was enough good in her to make up for them. But that night I realized I'd bought in to a lie, and I promised myself I would never compromise my values like that again. Instead, I would wait until I found the right person, even if that meant I stayed single the rest of my life."

He rocked back on the heels of his boots, struggling to find the right words. "Besides, I wasn't sure anyone would believe me. She painted a pretty stark picture of me. And, on top of that, what did it matter? We weren't getting married. My heart was broken, and I decided to simply walk away. But none of that matters anymore."

"It does to me." She stared out past him at the mountains. "I've held on to this grudge against you for all these years on false information."

"Honestly, I'm flattered you remembered me at all," he teased, trying to lighten the heaviness that had fallen between them.

"I'm serious, Caden."

"I know." He bit the edge of his tongue and started walking again. "I'm sorry."

"But that's just it. You had nothing to be sorry about. You *have* nothing to be sorry about. I just... Back then it was so hard for me to see a friend hurt, and now I know it was nothing but a bunch of lies. I still can't believe she'd do something like that to you."

"I was just as much to blame, I'm sure. She needed more than I could give her."

"But she never should have treated you that way. She lied about you."

"It's over, Gwen. I've moved on and, honestly, once I got over the shock of how I misread her, I realized I was better off without her. So can we forget about Cammie? Because I can think of a dozen things I'd much rather be talking about right now. So many things I want to show you—like this."

They stepped into the clearing. Tall grass surrounded the large mountain pond, while white clouds billowed above them. Memories surfaced of him and his brothers fishing in the summers and skating on the ice in the winter.

I want to make memories with you now, Gwen…

"Wow…this is so beautiful," she said.

Like you.

Gwen stood next to him, taking in the view of the trees reflecting in the water and the mountains in the distance. "And I agree. There are plenty of other things we can be talking about. Like you and your father's idea. If you could come up with a solid business proposition, I have a lot of contacts—"

"I was thinking of something more…personal."

"Personal?"

He took a step toward her. Surely she was feeling what he was. "Something that has to do with you and me. Because I'm not wanting a business partner right now. I want you."

She looked up at him with those wide blue eyes that left him stumbling over his words.

"These—these last couple months of getting to know you made realize that I want you in my life as more than just a friend." He drew in a deep breath, wishing the words didn't sound so awkward. "I'm in love with you, Gwen."

"I don't know what to say."

"Say you feel the same way. That talking to me over the past few months hasn't been just about our shared experience, but because you feel the same things that I do." He tried to read her expression. "And now that you know that truth about Cammie…"

"I know I've been pushing you away because I was

so afraid you'd walk out on me like you did to Cammie."

"And I was afraid to trust you. But I have no intention of walking out on you. And unless I'm totally off base about us and what's going on…"

She hesitated before reaching up and putting her arms around his neck, then she kissed him.

His mind spun, as if she was bringing light to the broken crevices of his heart for the first time. The healing they both needed.

She pulled away a few inches from him, smiling. "Does that clear things up for you a little bit? Because I'm in love with you too, Caden O'Callaghan."

"A lot, actually, because I was so afraid of what your reaction would be."

"That could have made a very awkward weekend together, which I would hate." She sounded breathless as she looked up at him. "Do I need to prove it to you again?"

"You might have to."

"What about your family?" she asked, brushing her lips against his. "What are they going to think about me? I'm sure they've heard the story of Cammie and the things I said to you. They probably have some reservations about me."

He pulled her back against him. "For one, I never told my family all the details, but I'm not really thinking about my family right now."

Her smile widened. "Then what are you thinking about?"

"I'm thinking about the two of us starting something more…permanent together."

His pulse raced as she looked up at him.

"I think I like the sound of that, Caden O'Callaghan."

He pulled her closer. "Good. Because I've finally found the person I want to spend the rest of my life with."

* * * * *

If you enjoyed this thrilling story from Lisa Harris,
watch for Reid's book later this year.

And don't miss the other
O'Callaghan brothers' stories:

Sheltered by the Soldier
Christmas Witness Pursuit

Available now from Love Inspired Suspense.

Find more great reads at www.LoveInspired.com.

Dear Reader,

Thank you so much for joining me on Caden and Gwen's journey! I loved exploring their new relationship, especially with such conflicting pasts. Have you ever been in a situation where you had to face the consequences of lies and secrets? Maybe they were your own secrets, or maybe they were someone else's, but either way the results can be devastating. And it can leave you feeling lost and alone. Jesus talks about being free, and how true freedom from whatever might be in your past comes through him. Let him be your refuge and your fortress!

Be sure you don't miss the next page-turning suspense story from Timber Falls and the O'Callaghan brothers!

Lisa Harris

SPECIAL EXCERPT FROM

LOVE INSPIRED SUSPENSE
INSPIRATIONAL ROMANCE

They must work together to solve a cold case...
and to stay alive.

Read on for a sneak preview of
Deadly Connection *by Lenora Worth,*
the next book in the True Blue K-9 Unit: Brooklyn *series,*
available June 2020 from Love Inspired Suspense.

Brooklyn K-9 Unit officer Belle Montera glanced back on the shortcut through Cadman Plaza Park, her K-9 partner, Justice, a sleek German shepherd, moving ahead of her as she held tightly to his leash. She had a weird sense she was being followed, but it had to be nothing.

Justice lifted his black nose and sniffed the humid air, then gave a soft woof. He might have seen a squirrel frolicking in the tall oaks, or he could have sensed Belle's agitation. Still on duty, she kept a keen eye on her surroundings.

"No time to go after innocent squirrels," she told Justice. "We're working, remember?"

Her faithful companion gave her a dark-eyed stare, his black K-9 unit protective vest cinched around his firm belly.

They were both on high alert.

"It's okay, boy," she said, giving Justice's shiny black-and-tan coat a soft rub. "Just my overactive imagination getting the best of me."

She had a meeting with a man who could have information regarding the McGregor murders. The DNA match from that case had indicated that US marshal Emmett Gage could be related to the killer.

The team had done a thorough background check on the marshal to eliminate him as a suspect, then Belle had been assigned to meet with him.

Justice lifted his head and sniffed again, his nose in the air. The big dog glanced back. Belle checked over her shoulder.

No one there.

She slowed and listened to hear if any footsteps hit the strip of pavement curving through the path toward the federal courthouse near the park.

Belle heard through the trees what sounded like a motorcycle revving, then nothing but the birds chirping. Minutes passed and then she heard a noise on the path, the crackle of a twig breaking, the slight shift of shoes hitting asphalt, a whiff of stale body odor wafting through the air. The hair on the back of her neck stood up and Belle knew then.

Someone is following me.

Don't miss
Deadly Connection *by Lenora Worth,*
available June 2020 wherever
Love Inspired Suspense books and ebooks are sold.

LoveInspired.com